MIDDLE SCHOOL

RAFE'S AUSSIE MISADVENTURE

Also by James Patterson

For more information about James Patterson's novels, visit
www.jamespatterson.co.uk

Or become a fan on Facebook

MIDDLE SCHOOL

RAFE'S AUSSIE MISADVENTURE

JAMES PATTERSON

AND MARTIN CHATTERTON

RANDOM HOUSE AUSTRALIA

To Mortimer and Agnetha DeVere,
the ultimate middle school survivors
—M.C.

A Random House book
Published by Random House Australia Pty Ltd
Level 3, 100 Pacific Highway, North Sydney NSW 2060
www.randomhouse.com.au

Penguin
Random House
RANDOM HOUSE BOOKS

First published by Random House Australia in 2015

Random House Books is part of the Penguin Random House group of companies whose addresses can be found at global.penguinrandomhouse.com.

National Library of Australia
Cataloguing-in-Publication Entry

Creator: Patterson, James, 1947—
Title: Rafe's Aussie adventure/James Patterson, Martin Chatterton.
ISBN: 978 0 85798 601 6 (pbk)
Series: Middle school; 7.
Target Audience: For primary school age.
Subjects: Middle schools—Juvenile fiction.
Adventure stories.
Other Creators/Contributors: Chatterton, Martin, author.
Dewey Number: 813.54

Cover illustration by Martin Chatterton
Cover design by Christabella Designs
Typeset by Midland Typesetters, Australia
Printed in Australia by Griffin Press, an accredited ISO AS/NZS 14001:2004 Environmental Management System printer

Random House Australia uses papers that are natural, renewable and recyclable products and made from wood grown in sustainable forests. The logging and manufacturing processes are expected to conform to the environmental regulations of the country of origin.

CHAPTER 1

ZOMBIE INVASION!

You know that icky feeling you get in the pit of your stomach when you look out of your bedroom window at night and see a mob of bloodthirsty Australian zombies heading right at you?

No?

Well, I'm here to tell you that seeing a whole bunch of the walking dead making a beeline for yours truly was definitely NOT one of my better moments. And for any of you who've been keeping up with all things Khatchadorian, you'll know that there has been a *ton* of weirdness in my recent history.

From the look on their crummy, dirt-streaked,

bug-eyed faces and the nasty collection of homemade weapons they were waving around— pitchforks, tennis rackets, flaming torches, barbecue tongs, a rusty exhaust pipe from a 2006 Holden, a viciously spiked fin off of a surfboard— these dudes were serious about claiming top spot in Rafe Khatchadorian's All-Time Disaster list.

I don't mind admitting I was a teeny-tiny bit FREAKED OUT.

The zombie dudes had made a real effort too. Do you have any idea how *hard* it would be to find a pitchfork these days? No, me neither, but it must be pretty difficult. The fact that this mob had come up with THREE of the things showed a real level of zombie determination. No howling mob is complete without pitchforks.

Despite the worrying presence of pitchforks, there was, however, one small ray of hope that I clung on to: Maybe it wasn't me they were after. It could be that the zombies had other fish to fry besides Rafe Khatchadorian of Hills Valley.

That hope faded quickly when they started chanting: "WE WANT RAFE! WE WANT RAFE!"

I guess that settled it. The seriously messed-up truth was that these guys wanted BLOOD—and lots of it. Very specifically, they wanted *my* blood, which was a real worry. I *like* my blood. Call me selfish, but I want to keep as much of my blood as I possibly can, for as long as I can.

In a weird way, though, a small part of me was kind of proud. It takes a lot to make that many Australian zombies mad, but I, Rafe Khatchadorian, had managed it in just a few short weeks. Ta-da!

Three weeks ago I didn't know a single person in Australia, let alone a zombie, and now I had a baying mob of the undead at the front door. Not bad when you think of it that way.

Oh, and just in case you think I'm going to turn around and tell you that this was all a dream—relax. I'm as guilty as anyone when it comes to the lame "it was all a dream" bohunkus (see *Save Rafe!*, one of my award-winning books) but this habit has to stop at some point and now seems like as good a time as any.

This was no dream. This all *happened*, straight up.

I'm Rafe, by the way. On a good day—like, a *really* good day—I look like this:

But usually it's more like this:

Okay, you're probably thinking all this zombie stuff is super-exciting and majorly awesome blah, blah, blah, Rafe, but why should we listen to a single word you say?

Sez you.

Ursula LeBon, book critic

Yeah, who do you think you are, Khatchadorian?

I'm so angry I could crush a grape!

He's talking voodoo!

And in reply I'd say this: Relax, readers. Draw your chairs in closer, remove persons of a nervous disposition from the vicinity and pin back your earflaps because we are about to go back, back through the mists of time, back to the very beginning, back to Hills Valley Middle School . . .

CHAPTER 2

THE GREAT
HERNANDEZ MUSTACHE
THEORY

We'll get to the zombies later because the BIG news at the *start* of this story isn't mutant flesh-eaters, it's that (drum roll, please!) I, Rafe Khatchadorian, have managed to stay enrolled at Hills Valley Middle School for more than a minute.

That's right, you heard me. Since we last spoke, I have NOT been expelled. Not even suspended! Detention, I hear you ask? Well . . . let's not go that far. I could be stuck in school for a million years.

But for me, not getting kicked out of school is *seriously* awesome, bordering on miraculous and hunkering down right next door to flat-out impossible.

It only seems like yesterday when the seriously scary new Vice Principal at Hills Valley, the knuckle-crunching Charlotte P. Stonecase (aka The Terror from Room 666 aka The Skull Keeper), forced me to take part in The Program, a kind of prison camp in the woods for "wayward students".

"Wayward" was a category I slotted into just fine, so before I could say, "No, wait, I think there's been some kind of mistake", I was shipped off to the Rocky Mountains for a week of *total* attitude realignment.

For a while there it was touch and go, but somehow I survived and made it back from Colorado alive.

Who knows, maybe the bottom line is that VP Stonecase wasn't so far off the mark about what I needed. Maybe she's some sort of cosmic fortune-teller.

Guru Stonecase

Anyway, this whole not-getting-into-major-trouble-at-Hills-Valley-Middle-School situation was so *weird* that I was convinced the school had been taken over by pod creatures. You know what I mean? The kind of aliens who sneakily replicate everyone until you're the only human left.

I decided to test my theory.

The big mistake I made was to test it by pulling Mr. Hernandez's mustache in gym class. You can already see where this is going, right?

Mr. Hernandez was standing in for Mr. Lattimore, our regular gym teacher, and I had some sort of brain-melt idea that pod people might use false mustaches or something. Looking back on it, I don't know why I thought the aliens would be okay replicating every other single thing about a person but would struggle with mustaches.

Now, in the short time he'd been at HVMS, us students had come to learn that Mr. Hernandez was not what you'd call the

Man! I just can't get this whole mustache thing!

forgiving type. In fact, trying to test the theory that Mr. Hernandez might be an alien pod person by doing what I did would normally have resulted in (at least) a hundred years of detention in the Hills Valley Middle School High Security Penitentiary and Mr. Hernandez mutating into a black hole of vengeance.

But things were so *weird* that Mr. Hernandez only made me run twenty laps of the football field.

Like I say—*weird*. And we haven't even got to the drop bears.

CHAPTER 3

BUDGIE SMUGGLERS, AHOY!

Later that day, things got even weirder.

The school had a special assembly, and after Principal Stricker had droned on a bit like she does, she introduced the Mayor of Hills Valley.

Mayor Blitz Coogan is one of those big, nice, friendly guys who slaps everyone on the back in a big, nice, friendly way with his gigantic paws. He gave Principal Stricker such a big, nice, friendly pat on the back that she almost coughed up a lung and crowd-surfed off the stage.

"G'day, Hills Valley!" Mayor Coogan boomed into the microphone. "Fair dinkum it's a bonzer arvo for you and yer cobbers to put on the old budgie smugglers and take the planks down the beach to catch a couple of goofy breaks out back!"

There was a stunned silence.

Other than the words "Hills Valley", nothing Mayor Coogan had said made any sense. The principal (and most of us) looked at the Mayor like he'd lost his mind. Mayor Coogan just stood there smiling like a guy who'd won the lottery.

"I just got back from a trip to Shark Bay, Australia, where my brother, Biff, lives. That's what folks in Australia speak like! And I've got some very exciting news—Mayor Coogan paused again like he was announcing the winner of a national TV talent show—"Hills Valley is now *twinned* with Shark Bay!"

Mayor Coogan beamed a big, beamy smile that made him look as though a xylophone was lodged in his mouth and waited for the applause to die down. The only problem was that there wasn't any, other than a few claps from the teachers.

The only way it could have been any worse was if his pants had fallen down.

"Twinning," Mayor Coogan continued, "is about a lot of things."

It was all about reaching out. It was all about sharing ideas. It was all about cultural exchange.

It was all so boring I almost passed out.

Until something Mayor Coogan said jolted me out of my drooly burger daydream.

". . . and first prize in the Shark Bay/Hills Valley Art Prize will be a three-week all-expenses-paid trip to Australia. Judging takes place next week. Get creative, Hills Valley, and you could be on that plane!"

Art, I thought. I can do art.

I could win that prize! I bet Mom would like that A LOT.

Let's just say I haven't had a great relationship with HVMS, which has been hard on Mom, too. Mostly because they have a rule book so big that it requires two grown men to open it. And also because I, um, got expelled at one point.

Being expelled isn't a good look for anyone, so winning Mayor Coogan's art prize could give me *another* another chance at a fresh start.

Besides, Mom deserved a break. Bringing up a problem-attracting doofus like me—as well as my annoying brainiac little sister, Georgia—can't be easy on your own.

REASONS TO ENTER
THE ART PRIZE
① THREE **WHOLE** weeks off School.
② THREE **WHOLE** weeks away
from Georgia.
③ THREE **WHOLE** weeks without
Miller the Killer.
④ THREE **WHOLE** weeks for
Jeanne Galletta to realise
how much she misses me.
⑤ I get to go to Australia.

So, if I'm such a good artist and I have a shot at a free trip Down Under, and if winning that trip would massively please Mom and make her life just that bit easier, why did I have a feeling in my stomach like I'd just swallowed an octopus?

CHAPTER 4

FAIR TRADE

Mayor Coogan's speech lasted longer than
the last Ice Age, so I'll condense it down
to the bare bones.

Shark Bay is a surfing town a few hours north
of Sydney. The idea was that the winner of the
art prize would head Down Under to have an
exhibition there and an Australian artist would
come over to Hills Valley to do the same thing.
Now, I had no idea about what Shark Bay was like,
and I don't want to beat up my own hometown, but
that didn't sound like much of a trade.

An expert panel—Mayor Blitz Coogan,
Ms. Donatello (the Hills Valley Middle School
art teacher), and Earl O'Reilly of Earl's Auto (the
sponsor of the prize)—would make the decision.

Someone tapped me on the shoulder. It was
Ms. Donatello.

"You should give it a shot," she said. "I think you have a real chance, Rafe."

Ms. Donatello is always doing stuff like that. She's a bit like my mom in that way—saying I can do things, even when I'm not too sure I can. It kind of freaks me out but in a good way, if you know what I mean.

"Or don't you want a free trip to Australia?"

Ah. Now that was a question. Who *wouldn't* want a trip to Australia? Beaches, sun, shrimps on the barbie, palm trees . . . er . . . kangaroos. But even though Ms. Donatello had a good point, that octopus in my guts was still sloshing around like crazy.

Only I knew why.

Curse you, Discovery Channel!

CHAPTER 5

KILLER FRUIT

Flashback: Three days earlier, a Friday night.
My absolute favorite night of the week and
I was practising my favorite pastime: Kicking
Back In Front Of The TV With
A Bag Of Corn Chips. Turns
out I'm pretty good at it.

Georgia was out doing little-sister stuff somewhere with her little-sister friends, and Mom was making something tasty-smelling in the kitchen. I settled into the cushions, put my feet up, and switched on the TV.

"Doesn't get much better than this, hey, Leo?" I shoveled another fistful of Tastee Taco Shells into my mouth. Leo didn't say anything. He had a mouth full of Tastee Taco Shells. Plus, he's imaginary.

These days he mostly sticks to showing up in my drawings. I mean, it's not like I'm *completely* nuts. Not yet, anyway.

I was watching a Discovery Channel special about—you guessed it—Australia. It was great. The reason it was so great was that, apparently, everything in Australia is dangerous. Everything. And when I say everything, I mean *everything* everything.

The flowers are toxic. *Flowers*.

The Lilshopohorroria (aka: The Pink Terminator)

Some of them, anyway. There's a fruit that tastes like paradise but contains vicious barbed hooks that latch onto the soft part of your throat, causing you to die. HOOKS! What possible reason could there be for a tasty fruit to contain killer throat hooks?!

The Irikandji, the world's most venomous jellyfish, lives in Australia. The thing looks like a transparent Gummy Bear. It was like the whole ecosystem had been designed by some complete nutzoid with a twisted sense of humor.

"Man," I muttered, "that is one scary place!" As far as I could tell, Australia was basically an island full of monsters.
They had birds that could *kill* you.

Why would a giant bird need claws?
It made no sense. The cassowary didn't
even fly. It only had little stunted wings.

Wouldn't it have been a better idea for the
cassowaries to have grown some proper wings
and left the claws and sprinting to the cheetahs?

Creature after creature rolled on-screen,
each of them even more fearsome, bloodthirsty,
or plain screwy than the last. Crocodiles as big
as school buses, Tasmanian devils (don't ask),
goannas (basically dinosaurs), vampire bats
(of course), stone fish (deadly fish sneakily
disguised as stones), poisonous blue-ringed
octopus (a cute little octopus that is possibly the
most poisonous creature on the planet), venomous
snakes by the bucketload, redback spiders,
scorpions, stick insects (so big they should be
called log insects), killer caterpillars (*caterpillars!*),
toadfish with teeth shaped like a parrot's beak that
can take off your toe . . . and sharks.

Lots and lots and lots of sharks. Tiger sharks,
bull sharks, makos, hammerheads, blues, and the
daddy of them all—the shark that gives
me nightmares—the Great White.

Nothing on earth could ever persuade me to set foot in Australia.

"They have sharks in America too, dummy," Leo said.

"Not in Hills Valley, they don't," I replied, and switched the channel to something more soothing—a show about your friendly neighborhood serial killer.

THAT OLD DONATELLO MIND-MELD JUJU

Okay, so we've established that there was absolutely no way, no how, no chance on this earth that I would even think about entering the Shark Bay/Hills Valley Art Prize.

And on Tuesday morning that's exactly what I didn't do—*think*.

Without knowing how, but most likely by Ms. Donatello's sneaky use of some evil alien mind-meld thing, I found myself bundling up my best drawings and sketchbooks, putting them into a folder, taking them into school, walking to the judging room, and submitting my drawings to the art prize committee.

As I closed the door on my way out, everything seemed to get sharper and clearer, as though the entire morning had taken place underwater. Ms. Donatello's mind-melding juju must have been more powerful than I thought.

It didn't really matter, though, I reflected on my way back to class. There was no way on earth *I'd* win. Stuff like that doesn't happen to me. Rafe Khatchadorian is the kid who gets busted, the kid who stuffs things up, the kid who is stalked by Miller the Killer through the halls of Hills Valley, the kid who, above all else, *fails*.

But perhaps there was an alignment of the planets or something—Mars rising above Uranus, or the Mayan calendar readjusting—because . . . I won.

That's correct. A trip to Australia, all expenses paid! An exhibition in Shark Bay! Best of all, THREE WEEKS OFF SCHOOL!

THRee. WHOLe. weeks.

Khatchadorian shoots! He scores! He *WINS!* Is there *nothing* this kid can't do?

And then I remembered something. Something that put a crimp in my plans, something that meant the trip Down Under couldn't happen.

"You remembered the sharks, didn't you?" Leo said. Leo is sharp like that. He always knows exactly what I'm thinking, which isn't surprising since he lives inside my head.

"Uh-huh," I said. "And the snakes and spiders and crocodiles and jellyfish and octopus."

Leo shrugged. "You could always stay out of the ocean."

I was about to say what a dumb idea *that* was when I realized that Leo was right. I *could* stay out of the ocean. I can't remember hearing about anyone being eaten by a Great White while skateboarding. Staying out of the ocean would reduce my chances of being eaten by a Great White by at least 100 percent. I liked those odds a whole bunch better. It would mean abandoning my surfing plans, but you can't have everything.

"The snakes and spiders are probably not as bad as the Discovery Channel made out," Leo said. "TV exaggerates things, like, a million billion times."

Leo was right again. I *was* probably making too much of the creepy-crawlies. They were *bugs*. Okay, they might be bugs the size of a spaniel, and they might carry enough venom to stun a polar bear, but they were still just bugs. And what was the chance of actually *meeting* a snake?

"And if you still think Australia's too scary you could always say no," Leo said. "Hand back the prize."

Hand back the prize? I froze. Leo had a point.

A really *stupid* point.

"Are you out of your mind?" I yelled. "I *won* something! Me! There's no way I'm handing that back. Are you kidding? *Australia*, dude! Sun, beaches, first-class plane tickets, surfing, girls, koala bears, the Sydney Harbor Bridge, my very own exhibition, the Opera House!"

"Because you really like opera."

"I'm on a roll, Leo, and the only thing you can do when you're on a roll is—"

"Put butter on it?"

"Go with the flow!"

Leo looked puzzled. "How does that work? Going with the flow and being on a roll? Like, wouldn't you—"

"Don't worry about all that! I won. We're going. Everything's coming up roses for Rafe Khatchadorian!"

random reader

WOAH! HEY! STOP RIGHT THERE! TIME OUT! TIME! OUT!

Now, hold up, Khatchadorian! How is it that five minutes ago you were bleating about sharks and spiders and all that stuff, then—*bingo!*—now you're rolling over like a puppy getting its tummy rubbed and accepting the prize! What gives?

I'll tell you what gives, readers: Success!

It's not something I've had much of these past few years and now that things are going well for me—for once—I'm not about to let that go by. I might look stupid but I'm not *that* stupid.

I think this is where someone says, "No, you're not stupid, Rafe!" Anyone? Anyone? Hello?

People are noticing me now. Jeanne Galletta said I looked "interesting" in math class yesterday.

Earl O'Reilly told Mom that Hills Valley was very proud of me and that he was sure I'd do a great job of representing us to Austria and that I should be sure to get some good skiing in while I was over there (I think Earl may have some work to do on his geography skills). The *Hills Valley Sentinel* was even planning to do a story on me. On ME! I'm in the big leagues, baby!

Of all the reasons for going to Australia, though, the one that meant the most was my mom smiling so much when I told her that I thought her face would break.

"Rafe, you star!" she yelled, and gave me a great big embarrassing mom hug in the middle of Swifty's (the diner she works at). "My own little Picasso!"

I was going to make a joke about Picasso but I didn't want to ruin the moment. Plus, Mom would have grounded me.

And the sharks? I'll figure that out once I get over there.

CHAPTER 7

MUTANT ALBATROSS FEATHERS

I should have known there'd be a catch. A big Mom-shaped catch.

"*Of course* I'm coming with you. If you think they'd let someone your age fly halfway around the world and hang out in a foreign country alone, then you have another think coming, mister!"

Well, you could have knocked me down with a feather. In fact, just as Mom handed out this shocking bit of news, a feather from a passing mutant albatross hit me on the shoulder and I went down like a boxer in the tenth round.

Okay, I might have been exaggerating that albatross thing a little—in the sense that it didn't happen—but you have to cut me some slack here. Finding out that Mom was coming with me Down Under was a heavy blow.

When you're my age, going *anywhere* with your mom—even if she's a good one like mine—is about as uncool as you can possibly get. Had I really imagined she'd let me fly solo halfway around the world and hang out alone in a foreign country doing exactly what I wanted, when I wanted, and where I wanted?

You bet!

When Mom broke the terrible, terrible news that she was going to be coming with me, I didn't lie around whining— I stood up to do my whining like a man! I whined in the living room, I whined in the lounge, and I whined in the kitchen. I whined before breakfast and I whined at dinner.

I whined from dawn to dusk with scarcely a break for breathing. I whined like no kid has ever whined before.

The Khatchadorian DEATH STARE

And I didn't restrict myself to whining. I moaned, pleaded, begged, sulked, shouted and whimpered . . . all producing exactly zero results. I even pulled out my secret weapon and gave Mom the full-beam patented Khatchadorian Death Stare which has been known to cut a hole in two-inch titanium, but Mom just asked me if I had something in my eye and to quit blocking the TV.

I cut my losses and stomped off to my room and stayed there for a long, long time.

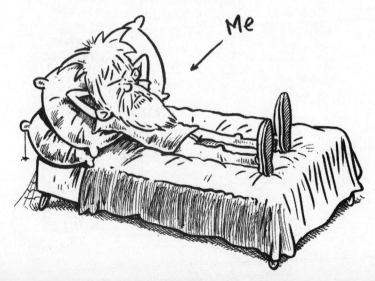

Me

By the eve of The Trip, I had adapted to the idea of being papoose boy Down Under. It wasn't like I was happy about it, but I had moved on from whine to whatever.

After a restless night plagued by croc-infested dreams, I woke at dawn. I already felt jet-lagged and I hadn't even gotten out of bed.

I'll spare you all the details about Mom wailing like a wounded hyena when saying goodbye to Georgia and Grandma Dotty. It was gross. There was enough salt water splashing about to fill the Hills Valley Municipal Swimming Pool with plenty left over but, eventually, we got on the plane.

Welcome to Aussie Airways, mates! I'm your captain, Ryan "Mad Dog" Porter. Today we'll be cruising at an altitude of, like, real high. Due to the lack of space on board there will be no meals served but the cabin crew will hurl stale bags of peanuts at you and you can fight it out among yourselves...

TUNA

AUSSIE

That's when we noticed that Earl and the Mayor hadn't exactly splashed out on the plane tickets.

But despite the plane, and despite Mom coming along, I decided I was just going to enjoy Australia. I wedged myself happily into the window seat and watched the Pacific unfurl below me. I was a new Rafe Khatchadorian, a globetrotting Rafe Khatchadorian, an internationally famous artist Rafe Khatchadorian.

It would be fine. What could possibly go wrong?

CHAPTER 8

THE BEAST

I was right on the crest of The Beast—a wave so big that some of the surf pros were having second thoughts about going back out again.

The seatbelt light pinged and I woke up sweating like a pizza-munching pig in a sauna.

I think I may have been talking in my sleep because I noticed a couple of passengers with their fingers hovering over the FLIGHT ATTENDANT button on their armrests. I shifted slightly in my seat.

Hey! I'm just big-boned!

"Quit moving around so much," Mom hissed, clutching my arm. "You'll make the plane wobble."

I glanced at her tray table. Did I mention she's not a good flyer? No? Okay, well the truth is that she is possibly The Most Nervous Passenger in The History of Flying.

Spread out across her table was a rabbit's foot, a four-leaf clover, a Bible, a copy of the Qur'an, a sprig of heather, a string of prayer beads, a silver cross of St. Christopher, two sick bags, a "lucky" pebble shaped like Minnesota that Mom had found in the yard, a laminated copy of the plane safety features, a bottle of AbsoCalm travel pills, a book by Dr. Enrique Meloma titled *Don't Freak Out at 35,000 Feet Ever Again!*, and a picture of the Dalai Lama.

I looked out of the window and immediately
forgot all about my dream. (That's right, that
wave and shark stuff was all a dream. I won't do
it again, promise.) The plane was coming in low
over a perfect blue sea. We'd arrived in Australia
and it was all I could do to stay in my seat.

As we touched down and coasted alongside
a strip of trees that lined the edge of the bay,
I pressed my nose against the window and caught
a glimpse of something furry moving in the upper
branches. I looked closer and saw a flash of light as
the sun winked off the creature's eyes. I swear it
was staring at me.

"Did you see that?" I said to Mom, but she had her eyes screwed shut and her hands clamped so tightly on the armrests that it was a miracle they were still in one piece. "Mom! I saw something in the trees!"

A deep voice came from behind my left shoulder and I jumped about six feet. It was the man in the row behind me, leaning forward.

"You saw something, son?" he said with a strong Australian accent. His face was leathery, and his blond hair was greying at the sides. He had the air of a man who wrestled crocodiles for fun.

I nodded. "In the trees."

"Drop bears," the man said gravely.

I saw the woman next to him glance at him quickly. "Terry . . ." she said.

"The boy's got to know, Shirl," the man said in a voice that came all the way from down in his boots. "He's a visitor to our country."

Shirl shook her head and turned back to her magazine.

The man leaned forward as the plane taxied toward the terminal. His voice dropped to a whisper. "That was a drop bear you saw, son."

"A drop bear?" I said. "I've never heard of them."

"That's what they want," the man replied, although he never said who this mysterious "they" were. "Drop bears are the most dangerous animal in Australia. They call 'em koalas to throw you off the trail. I used to hunt them on the Sydney Harbor Bridge. Every night they'd climb up there and cling to the steel—they like the warmth, you see—and every now and again one would drop down to hunt. They kill hundreds every year. Just drop down and rip out their brains while they're still alive. Horrible, it is, just horrible."

"Hundreds of what?" I gasped. "What do they kill?" The Discovery Channel had obviously missed something out in their research.

There was a pause before he spoke, like he was weighing up whether or not to give me some very bad news. "Tourists," the man growled. "They feed on tourists, son."

I gasped. *I* was a tourist.

"That's enough, Terry," Shirl said.

The plane came to a halt and the UNFASTEN SEATBELT sign pinged on.

Terry unbuckled his seatbelt, his face grim. "You take care, sonny," he said. "Watch the skies and remember to take precautions."

"What sort of precautions?" I asked, but he'd gone.

CHAPTER 9

SHE'LL BE RIGHT, MATE

Australia is hot.

Like, REALLY hot. Frying-eggs-on-the-sidewalk hot. Ice-cream-melting-before-you-can-take-the-first-lick hot. Did I mention it was hot?

Is it me, or is it hot in here?

It was so hot that all thoughts of drop bears vanished. Having my brains sucked out and eaten would be the least of my problems. I'd be boiled alive *long* before that happened.

Hey, Hills Valley has had hot days—plenty of them—but there was one small but VERY important detail I had forgotten. While it was winter back home, here in Upside-Down Land it was most definitely summer.

"This is nice," Mom said, smiling.

I looked at her like she'd gone crazy. Somehow, between leaving the plane and getting outside, and without me noticing a thing, she had magically changed into light summer clothes. How do they *do* that? Moms, I mean.

"Nice?" I replied, my voice dripping with acid. *"Nice?"*

I had expected Australia to be warm, but this was something else. People needed Special Forces training to deal with this kind of thing. How did Australians stop themselves from melting? Did they have some sort of force field? Ice water running through their veins? Skin like elephant hide? Whatever it was, I needed to find out—and soon.

To make matters worse, the airline had lost our bags.

"Once we find 'em we'll send 'em up to Shark Bay," the smiling, blond surfer-type guy said from behind the desk. "She'll be right, mate."[1]

---

1 "She'll be right, mate" = "I have absolutely no idea what the outcome of this problem might be, up to and including injury and/or death (for you), but I'm blindly hoping that things will turn out for the best." Never trust an Australian who says this to you.

What I found out in Australia was that quite often things did not turn out right but—and this is the important thing to remember—it never stops them from saying it. Be warned. And, no, I don't know why it's always "she" who'll be right and not "he". It just is.

The second thing that happened (after losing our bags) was that the trip north to Shark Bay was going to take SEVEN HOURS.

On a bus with a malfunctioning air-con.

Seven.

HOURS.

A TV at the front of the bus was switched to the news. The grinning anchorman proudly told us that Australia was experiencing one of the hottest days on record with the mercury nudging 46 degrees Celsius. The guy sounded proud, like it was something to boast about.

"That's one hundred and fifteen degrees Fahrenheit!" I gasped. "Seven hours without air-con?" I asked the driver.

"She'll be right, mate," he replied, smiling like a chimpanzee with a caffeine problem.

See?

I'll spare you the full horror of the journey.

All you need to know is that at one point a bug as big as a bear flew across my face and, instead of screaming like a normal person, I was just grateful for the breeze.

When we arrived at our first rest stop, I staggered down the steps of the bus. Wherever we'd stopped was hotter than Sydney. I was literally melting.

I was about to complain, but after seeing Mom's jet-lagged expression, I stopped melting and got back on the bus. Moms can do that—stop people from melting, I mean.

At least I didn't see any more drop bears in the trees. It was probably too hot, even for them.

CHAPTER 10

THUNDER DOWN UNDER

When the bus arrived in Shark Bay, the boiling day had curdled into a full-scale thunderstorm. Rain of biblical proportions hammered down on the roof of the bus.

I gazed out the window and nudged Mom. "Look at that."

Outside, palm trees were bending in the wind. It was like the news footage you see when Channel Z is reporting from Miami or Haiti. I saw a small car tumbling through the air followed by a pizza shop and what looked like a whole herd of cows.

Okay, I made that last bit up. But it did look bad.

"I hope it's not a hurricane," Mom said. She leaned forward and tapped the driver on the shoulder. "This isn't a hurricane or something we should be worried about, is it?" She paused, then added, "We're American."

"Nah, just a bit of a breeze," the bus driver said. "Anyway, we don't believe in hurricanes. In Australia we have cyclones."

"Isn't a cyclone just another name for a hurricane?" I asked.

My nights in front of the Discovery Channel had included plenty of stuff on typhoons, tsunamis, hurricanes, and tornadoes. I was something of an expert now.

"Nah," the driver said, looking at me as if I was nuts. "*Totally* different thing. She'll be right, mate."

"What about those hailstones?" Mom said.

"Those itty-bitty little specks of ice? Completely flamin' harmless! Now get off me flamin' bus, ya drongos!"

That's not how this guy— or any actual Australian— talks, but at this point that's what it sounds like to Rafe. Go with it.

The bus driver skidded to a halt in what looked like the parking lot of a fried chicken joint in Hills Valley. The rain had turned to hail and we made a run for a bus shelter. We had gone from super-hot to ice-cold in less than two minutes. We had clearly found ourselves in the middle of some enormous natural disaster.

The bus driver had obviously escaped from a mental-health facility. What he'd done with the real bus driver I didn't like to think about. The best we could hope for was that our water-logged bodies would be found wedged in the branches of a tree a week later during the massive clean-up operation.

Over the noise of the hailstones hammering down, Mom told me that Mayor Coogan's brother, Biff, was supposed to meet us. I leaned against a graffiti-covered wall and looked out at the curtain of hail.

'This isn't what I'd imagined,' I said, but Mom wasn't listening.

She was fast asleep.

CHAPTER 11

CHUNDER DOWN UNDER

After what seemed like hours, but was actually six minutes and eighteen seconds, a car screeched into the parking lot and slid to a halt in front of the bus shelter. A man-sized chicken sprang out of the driver's seat and stood looking at us as hailstones the size of tennis balls bounced off his head as though they were made of popcorn.

Maybe the hail *was* popcorn. Nothing would surprise me about Australia. For all I knew the hailstones contained exploding poison darts, or possessed claws, or six sets of fangs. Everything else in this country seemed to have unnecessary protective armor.

Or the chicken possibly had a head made of solid granite.

Either way, he didn't seem to notice.

The chicken's car, on the other hand, took a beating. I watched a wing mirror get caught by a particularly large hailstone and crash to the ground. Ice *rat-a-tat-tatted* the roof, and the windscreen cracked in three places. The chicken didn't seem to mind. Maybe these giant chickens had plenty of spare cars.

"G'day, you blokes!" the chicken boomed. He lifted his wings and pulled off his head to reveal someone who looked very much like Blitz Coogan. "Biff Coogan's the name, and I'm mayor of this joint!" Biff Coogan pointed at his chicken suit. "I don't normally dress like this, but me and Mrs. Coogan have got a fancy-dress party coming up and I've been to pick up my

costume. Thought I'd leave it on and give you
a bit of a laugh!"

"Ha ha," I said, doing my best.

It seemed to satisfy Biff.

"What about your car?" I asked. "Aren't
you . . .?"

Biff glanced at the car. "Oh, that's not mine.
It's Mrs. Coogan's. My car had a bit of a run-in
with the hailstones, but this car's a beaut.
She'll—"

"Let me guess," I said. "She'll be right, mate?"

"You got it, buddy," said Biff. 'We'll make an
Aussie of you yet!"

It was obvious he'd been in Australia a long time. Any trace of an American accent had gone. He sounded more Australian than any of the Australians we had met so far.

He stepped forward and shook Mom's hand.

"Ha!" she said. "I mean, hi. Ny mane'th Rafe and this son is my Jules. I mean, my name's Rafejools and this son is my. Wait, what I mean—"

She might have been trying to *look* like she wasn't auditioning for a role in a zombie flick, but, sure as sharks have teeth, she wasn't succeeding. She sounded as if her tongue had been replaced by a drowsy ferret.

Biff didn't seem to notice.

"No worries, Rafejools! Welcome to Australia!" Biff opened the doors to what was left of Mrs. Coogan's car. "Pity we couldn't have fixed up some sun for you guys. Okay, let's go!"

We made a death-defying leap through the hail and into the relative safety of the back seat. The noise inside the car was even louder than in the bus shelter. Biff looked round at us.

"You blokes are traveling light!" he yelled.

I didn't bother explaining. I was too tired. The bags would turn up or they wouldn't. After twenty-six hours on the move, plus a sleepless night before that, I didn't care if the bags ended up in Saskatchewan.

I sat back and watched as we drove through town. A sign read WELCOME TO SHARK BAY, AUSTRALIA'S MOST FEARLESS TOWN.

"Most fearless?" I said. "What's that all about?"

"Shark Bay surfers," Biff replied. "We got sharks here in Shark Bay—lots of sharks—but that never stops a Shark Bay surfer!"

I gulped and exchanged a meaningful look with Leo.

"Did he say 'lots'?" Leo asked.

I nodded.

"Oh boy."

"But don't worry," Biff said, "hardly anyone gets eaten. Heh, heh, heh, heh, heh."

"Great," I muttered. "How far to the hotel?" All I wanted was a shower and a bed I could sleep in for, say, three weeks straight.

"Oh, you'll be staying at our little beach shack," Biff said as he swerved round a tree in the middle of the road. He turned in his seat and grinned. "More cosy than a hotel, hey?"

I sat up and looked at Leo.

A *shack*? That hadn't been part of the deal. I'd thought it'd be some swanky five-star resort, not some complete stranger's back bedroom.

"I didn't know about *this*!" I hissed.

"Of course, Rafe," Mom said. She had a strange, glassy expression on her face and her skin looked a bit green. I began to wonder about those travel pills she'd been popping on the plane. She had mentioned something about side effects.

"I mean, we don't know these people!"

"Mmm, yeah, apples," Mom said, nodding. Her eyes wobbled in different directions. "And oranges. Christmas stockings."

I looked at her. "Mom, are you okay?"

"What a strange question, Rafe. Of course I'm Wednesday."

And then, before anyone could stop her, Mom leaned forward and puked all over the back of Biff Coogan's head.

It was a full-on pedal-to-the-metal puke tornado, too, not a measly quarter or half-hurl. It was the real deal, chunks blown, projectile Vom City to the maximillion. It was messy. It was loud. It was *spewtastic*.

It was probably the single most awesome thing I'd ever seen.

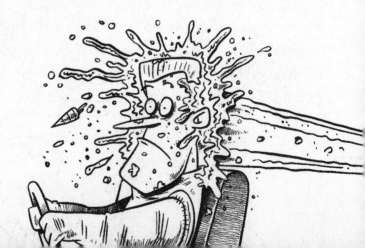

CHAPTER 12

BIFFZILLA VERSUS MOM

As you can imagine, the atmosphere inside the car cooled right down. In fact, the temperature dropped so much that you could have used the inside of the car as a training pod for an Antarctic expedition.

Everyone froze (I couldn't resist).

"Woah," I said. It seemed to sum up the situation.

Getting puked on by a complete stranger can't be much fun. Getting puked on by a complete stranger while dressed as a chicken must have been much, much worse.

And funnier, too, although a big part of me felt really (like, *really*) bad for Mom. She couldn't help herself, I wanted to say. I wanted to explain to Biff that a combination of jet lag, heat, travel pills, and an Aussie Airways tuna bake had combined to turn my polite mom into a walking puke machine, but Biff didn't look like he wanted anyone to talk to him, least of all me.

But, I thought, my hopes rising, we're in Australia. They have a different sense of humor to the rest of the world. They're used to sharks and snakes and poisonous flowers. Maybe being puked on was regarded as a bit of harmless fun Down Under?

No such luck. Biff wasn't giving even the slightest hint that any part of being puked on came within the same solar system of being "fun".

And—this is just a hunch—Mom puking on the mayor was probably the wrong way to start a cultural exchange. Right now, the chances of Hills Valley and Shark Bay becoming best buds looked about as likely as me playing football on the moon.

"I. Am. So. So. So. *So*. Sorry," Mom said. "*Really* sorry, Mayor Coogan. I couldn't help it."

She started trying to wipe the worst of the gunge off Biff's neck but only managed to squidge a chunky gloop of it right down the back of his chicken suit.

Biff squirmed out of her reach. He yanked a box of tissues toward him and began wiping the puke off by himself. Disregarding the hurricane outside, I wound down the window to let in some fresh air. I was beginning to feel a little pukey myself. I didn't think Biff would appreciate a repeat performance. Being puked on once is bad enough.

"She's been taking some travel pills," I shouted above the howling gale filling the car. "That must be it."

"If it's any consolation," Mom said, "I do feel a lot better now." Then she closed her eyes and fell fast asleep.

ZZZZZ!

A low rumbling noise, like someone dragging a heavy anchor over concrete, filled the car. It was loud enough to be clearly heard above the roar of the wind and hail. At first I thought we'd hit something and lost a tire and the noise was the wheel scraping across the road, but I realized it was Biff grinding his teeth. He was the angriest looking giant chicken I'd ever seen.

He said nothing, but I could tell by the vicious twist he gave the steering wheel to avoid a speedboat resting upside down in the middle of an intersection that he was about a millisecond away from turning round and putting us on the next bus back to Sydney. One more incident and I had no doubt that he'd mutate into a sort of Biffzilla and the whole Shark Bay/Hills Valley experiment would turn into a massive Khatchadorian-related disaster.

Oh no! It's Biffzilla!

I imagined slinking back home, a failure once more. It wasn't a good thought.

"Maybe we should take her to the hospital," Biff said, when he had finally unclenched his puke-spotted jaw.

"Nah," I replied. "She'll be right, mate."

I couldn't resist.

CHAPTER 13

IN THE BIG HOUSE

The Coogans' "shack" sprawled across most of the headland that wrapped around one end of Shark Bay. The moment we arrived the hail stopped. It was like someone had thrown a switch and the clouds were split by a beam of sunlight that lit up the place like a stage spotlight. I half-expected a choir of angels to start warbling.

Being a mayor must pay pretty well, because I'd seen smaller airports than Biff Coogan's beach shack.

In the driveway, a tall blond kid about my age stopped doing ollies on his skateboard and stared at me.

It wasn't a friendly look. His eyes reminded me of the drop bear.

"Brad, this is Ralph Katchadoorhandle," Biff said as he stepped out of the car. "Ralph, this is my son, Brad."

"Eew!" Brad said, pointing at Biff's puke-encrusted neck. "What in the name of Hugh Jackman's sideburns is *that* gunk?"

Biff shook his head and stomped toward the house.

"That's, er, puke," I said.

"You puked on Dad? Why?"

"No! My mom puked on your dad," I said, like that was okay.

Brad looked at me and then at Mom in the car. "But she's asleep."

"No," I said. "Well, yes, she is now, so she couldn't. But, no, she wasn't then, so she could have. And did. Puked, I mean."

Nope. Still not getting it, I am.

If I'm being honest, it wasn't the clearest answer I'd ever given. Even I could hardly understand it.

Brad opened his mouth to speak and then closed it again. You could almost see his brain trying to work out the sequence of events.

"Okay," he managed in the end. A blonde girl who looked a lot like Brad appeared next to him. I guessed she was Brad's twin sister. I'm quick like that.

"What's *that*?" she said, pointing at me like I was some sort of exotic slug. From the expression on her face I think she may have preferred the slug.

Brad shrugged. "Some American dude," he said. "Puked all over the old bloke. Fair dinkum."

"Ew, gross!"

"I didn't!" I protested.

"This is Belinda," Brad said.

Belinda looked at me briefly again and shook her head.

I wanted to tell her how tired we were and that it wasn't me who had puked on her dad, but I didn't have the energy. Instead, I opened my mouth and, without warning, puked all over Belinda.

CHAPTER 14

BEETROOT? *BEETROOT?*

Let's just say that Belinda took being puked on a lot worse than her dad.

For a moment there I thought she was going to beam me with Brad's skateboard, but her desire to clean my puke off her was too great. Belinda fled into the house, swearing undying hatred and vengeance against me in particular, and Americans in general.

I didn't blame her.

I would have felt exactly the same way if a random Australian showed up at Hills Valley and hurled chunks all over me. The fact that I couldn't help myself didn't mean zip.

Brad, on the other hand, thought it was the funniest thing he'd ever seen.

"Awesome," Brad said. He jumped onto his skateboard and disappeared down the driveway.

A few minutes later, after I'd got Mom out of the car, Mrs. Coogan stepped out the door. She must have heard all about the pukey Americans because I noticed she stayed a few paces out of hurl range.

Barb wasted no time showing us to our rooms and demonstrating exactly how the showers worked.

"Take your time," she said.

What Barb really meant...

You stink! Get cleaned up!

Thirty minutes later, showered and changed and feeling more like our old selves, we came downstairs to eat. I was dead tired and, surprisingly, very hungry. I imagined that we'd be eating giant cockroaches cooked on the barbie[2] or something, but we had regular steaks and burgers and fries and salad. The only weird thing was the beetroot Mrs. Coogan insisted on putting on the burger. Beetroot—I know.

Belinda didn't speak to me. I don't know if that would have been any different if I hadn't puked on her. I tried to apologize but got the brush-off.

A bunch of Brad and Belinda's friends came round for dinner. They were all just like them— all teeth and hair and tans. They were too good-looking, too tall, too fit, and too pleased with themselves. Going back to my well-established pod-people theories, this could only mean one thing: Brad and Belinda Coogan and all their friends were just too perfect to be human.

I think Mrs. Coogan thought having Brad and Belinda's friends there would make it easier for

---

2   There'll be more on weird Australian food later. You have been warned.

The REAL BRAD AND BELINDA!

me to become part of their little circle. If that
was the idea, it didn't look like it was going to
work. I hated Brad and Belinda's friends on
sight, and they hated me. It looked like Rafe
Khatchadorian was not going to be warmly
welcomed into the Shark Bay surfer community,
but I was so tired I didn't care. I just hoped that

not everyone in Australia would be like Brad and Belinda's crew.

By eight o'clock I could feel my eyes closing and Mom must have felt the same. We made our excuses and crawled to our rooms.

"Sleep tight, Rafe," Mom said as she opened her door.

I muttered something back but it might as well have been in Swahili. All I could think about was sleep, glorious sleep. I pushed open my bedroom door and looked at the bed with something like love.

Less than thirty seconds later I slid between the sheets, closed my eyes, and dropped off the edge of the world into the deepest sleep of my life.

CHAPTER 15

THE ROPE OF DOOM

There's *no* sleep like jet-lag sleep. It was like being under anesthetic. I sank into the soft billowing pillows, which soon turned into soft billowing clouds, and then I was gone. For a time there was just velvety blackness and then I began to dream I was tightrope-walking across a river. It wasn't a bad dream—the tightrope was wide and fat and warm beneath my feet. I wrapped my toes around the rope and kept walking.

The only trouble was that the wind started rising and the rope began moving up and down and from side to side. It became harder and harder for me to cling on, so I reached down and wrapped my arms tight around that rope and hung on as if my life depended on it. The rope was moving so much that it was wrapping itself around my legs and—

"This is not a drill, soldier! Mayday! I repeat, mayday!"

Leo's voice cut through my dream like a chainsaw through a meringue. My eyes popped open, but I couldn't see a thing in the darkened room. After a moment I realized that the tightrope was still moving.

That's weird, I thought. The tightrope was in my dream, wasn't it? How could it still be moving?

"The lights!" Leo screamed. "Hit the lights!"

I reached across and fumbled for the bedside lamp. My finger found the switch and I saw that the thing coiled around my feet and legs wasn't a tightrope.

It was a giant

SNAKE!

CHAPTER 16

REVENGE OF THE
TEENAGE POD PEOPLE

You know the movie *Snakes on a Plane*? This was *Snake in the Bed*. Much, much, *much* scarier. Mainly because it was happening to me in REAL LIFE and not to Samuel L. Jackson on a Hollywood movie set.

The snake and I stared at one another and time seemed to stop. Then, at incredible speed, a number of things happened all at once.

It is said by brainy scientists that it is aerodynamically impossible for a human being to fly. The laws of physics do not allow it.

And what I would say to those scientists is this: Quit flapping your gums, Einsteins. You might know plenty about science and mathematics, but

you don't know diddly squat about what a human is capable of when they find a snake in their bed. But if you wanted to conduct an experiment to find out, all you'd have to do was place one terrified teen (for the sake of argument, let's call him Rafe Khatchadorian) in close proximity to a giant snake, and you will see unaided human flight take place in about two seconds flat. Guaranteed.

Once I had computed the impossible information that there was, in fact, a snake in my bed, I levitated so fast that I bounced off the ceiling, spun around in midair, and rocketed out of the room at approximately 926 miles an hour without my feet touching the ground once.

Did I mention I was screaming?

Well, I was—loudly and without drawing breath and in a voice so high I was surprised the windows didn't shatter. As soon as I clapped eyes on the reptile in my bed I screamed like a police siren that didn't seem to have an OFF switch.

I screamed as I hurtled down the Coogans' landing, I screamed as I clattered down the stairs, and I was still screaming as I sprinted into the crowded living room, tripped over a coffee table and somersaulted into the TV, which exploded in a totally impressive shower of sparks and smoke. I was left sprawled half over the coffee table with my foot resting in a cake, my butt stuck up high in the air and my face buried in the carpet.

Even for me, it wasn't a good look.

See?

"SNNNNNNAAAAAAAAAAAAAAKKKKE!"
I howled, lifting my chin from the shag pile.
"S-S-S-S-S-S-S-S-S-SNAAAAAAAAAAKKKKKE!"

There was a moment of stunned silence. Biff
and Barb Coogan looked at me and then at the
busted TV.

"Snake?" I said. My voice went up at the end
of the word like I was asking a question (the
way Australians speak). Maybe I was turning
Australian. Maybe I *was* asking a question.
Maybe there hadn't been a snake?

Brad and Belinda and all their surfy-alien-
mutant friends laughed. They laughed until tears
ran down their perfect cheeks. They would stop
laughing for a second and then see my yellow
underwear with the space rockets and start
laughing all over again.

"Stop," one kid gasped, holding his hands up.
"I can't breathe!" And then he rolled over, his
shoulders shaking.

They'd stop laughing and then someone would
say, "The TV!" and off they'd go once more. If one
of them had literally laughed their head clean off
their shoulders I wouldn't have been surprised.

Even Biff and Barb joined in.

Then Mom arrived. "What's all the noise?" she asked.

"Rafe's making us all laugh," Barb Coogan said. "He's quite a joker, isn't he?"

Before Mom could reply, Brad turned to one of his friends. "You get that, Lachie?" he said.

I looked around to see Brad's friend holding up his phone and nodding. "Every last freakin' second, Bradster," he said. He leaned forward and high-fived Brad. "Uploading now."

CHAPTER 17

WHERE'S A GIANT
METEORITE
WHEN YOU NEED ONE?

'**D**id you scare
Dwickle
Rafey?' Brad said
in a singsong voice
as he scooped the
python from my
bed.

Shirley was so
big it took all of
Brad's strength to
lift the disgusting
thing. "I wondered
where you'd gone."

"Like you didn't know," I snarled.

"Rafe!" Mom cut in before Brad could reply. She put an arm around my shoulders. "Don't be silly, honey. You'd have to be mad to put a python in someone's bed."

"We-ll . . ." I muttered, but Mom didn't hear me. Perhaps it was for the best. She is usually someone who has my back, but she has this weird thing about being nice to people when you're staying in their home. In her book, being rude to a host is a big no-no. BIG no-no.

"Shirl wouldn't hurt a fly, Ralph," Biff said as Shirley draped herself around Brad's shoulders and went to sleep. "She's one of the family."

"Yeah?" I sneered. "I'm not a fly and the name's *Rafe*, not Ralph. Got it, boofboy?"

Or that's what I would have said if I'd had a spine.

My spine

slink slink

Instead, I just kind of grunted and stared at the floor, wondering when this would be over. I'd used up most of my dignity already, and winning an argument with someone whose TV you've just destroyed was always going to be difficult. And Biff probably hadn't quite forgotten about getting puked on by my mom.

Also, I was still only wearing my yellow boxer shorts. It's hard to get angry when all that stands between you and full-on public nudity is a scrap of thin cotton decorated with space rockets. It was chilly, too. A rain-cooled breeze was blowing in from Shark Bay and whistling right up my—

"Awesome!" Lachie held up his phone. "Seven hundred and fifty-five hits in three minutes. Man, this clip is clocking up some serious action!"

Everyone whooped.

Except me—and Mom, although I think I saw the beginnings of a smile around her mouth.

She patted me on the head. "Go and put some clothes on, sugar," she said quietly. "Try not to take it to heart. It'll all seem better in the morning."

I nodded even though I knew it wouldn't seem better in the morning. That was just the kind of thing that moms say. Mom meant well, but she hadn't looked deep into the shark eyes of the Coogan twins. If those androids had anything to do with it, my life would be worse in the morning. I slunk upstairs, turning back only when I heard them cackling like a bunch of hyenas in a laughing-gas factory.

Lachie stopped howling long enough to hold up the screen of his phone toward me. "I uploaded the whole clip, man!" he yelled, tears rolling down his face. "You should check it out. It's on completefails.com. The clip's called 'Classic Rafe Khatcha*dork*ian All-Time Snake Fail'."

"I wouldn't read the comments, dude,' Belinda said, looking up from her own phone.

I knew Belinda wasn't being kind. She was just letting me know that no matter how bad I thought the whole snake-screaming, TV-destroying humiliation had been, it was going to be a whole lot worse once everyone else on the planet had a chance to see it.

I left the room and stood miserably in the hallway.

A while back I'd seen a thing on TV about a giant meteorite the size of Wyoming being on a possible collision course with Earth. If it'd hit, we'd all have been wiped out in a split second.

Through a window set into the front door, I looked up hopefully at the Shark Bay night sky. Where was a giant meteorite when you needed one?

Gee, thanks, Belinda!

CHAPTER 18

T-REX ON THE ROOF

The next morning, it was as if everything that had happened the previous night had been a bad dream. Okay, my eyes felt like I'd been rinsing them with sand, my tongue had been replaced with what tasted like a dead rat, and I had cake crumbs wedged in areas I didn't know I had areas. But, other than that, I felt pretty good.

Outside, the sun glinted on waves rolling onto a curving mile of gleaming white sand. Behind the beach, the town of Shark Bay sparkled in the morning sun. The sky was blue and so was the crystal-clear water.

A pod of dolphins splashed in the surf. It was hot, but nothing like the cauldron of yesterday. Bright-green parrots screeched through the branches of the trees that edged the shimmering pool.

Other than Brad and Belinda, who were swimming laps, the view was pretty good. This trip might work out after all, I thought.

"Not too shabby, eh?" Leo said, and I had to agree.

I could get used to this.

Being an international jet-setting artist can be very tiring.

Other than a crane lifting a Tyrannosaurus Rex off the roof of a house a couple of streets away, there wasn't a trace of last night's storm.

"Back up a little there, cowboy," Leo said. "A *T-rex*?"

I jerked my head back toward the crane and saw that, despite no one in Shark Bay seeming even slightly concerned, it *was* actually a T-Rex being winched off the roof.

I was an expert on T-Rexes. By which I mean that I'd seen *Jurassic Park* and owned a purple plastic dinosaur Grandma Dotty had given me when I was six. Like I said, an expert.

"Oh, come on," I muttered. "You gotta be kidding."

CHAPTER 19

BAD NEWS AND MORE BAD NEWS

I had just opened my mouth, ready to start yelling "T-Rex!", when my super-spidey sixth sense kicked in and I shut my mouth like a shark on a surfer's leg. Another split second and I'd have started the day off by making a fool of myself *again*.

A T-Rex in downtown Shark Bay? Nuh-uh, don't think so.

Not even *I* was dumb enough to think that Australia still had dinosaurs, no matter how bitey and weird the rest of their animal population was.

I squinted at the crane and took a closer look. The T-Rex hung lightly from the crane, its arms and legs sticking stiffly out of the cradle wrapped around its belly. It was a fiberglass model from a nearby burger joint called Rex's Mightee Bites.

I nodded and wiped my brow. That had been a close call. I didn't want to lose any more cool than I already had. After last night I had very little reserves of cool left and the last thing I needed to do was blow it all in one false T-Rex panic.

I got dressed and went downstairs. Mom was sitting on the pool deck drinking coffee with Biff and Barb Coogan.

"Morning, Rafe," Mom said, smiling. "Isn't this place great?"

"Uh-huh." It was the best I could do for now.

Mom seemed to have smoothed things over with Biff. She's good at that—smoothing things over, I mean. One of her many mom skills. Yesterday she'd hurled chunks all over Biff. Now, less than twenty-four hours later, she was chatting to him like nothing had happened. I couldn't imagine Belinda being so forgiving with me.

my last can →

COOL

"You sssssssleeep okay?" Biff asked. "Pillowsss sssssssoft enough?"

I smiled weakly.

Mom leaned over and squeezed my hand. "He's only joking, Rafe. Isn't that right, Biff?"

"Yessss," Biff said. "Sssssssorry, Rafe. I won't sssssssay another word about sssnakes."

He was telling the truth. He didn't say a single word about snakes. Instead, he said lots of words *about* snakes. After about fifteen minutes of lame snake jokes from Biff, I eventually managed to get some breakfast.

"They'll get bored of all that snake stuff soon," Mom whispered to me. "Hang in there, honey. Today will be better, I promise."

"Okay," I said, and turned toward the table which was piled high with breakfast things. I hoped Mom was right. I could use some "better" today.

If the day was going to be an improvement on yesterday it didn't get off to a good start when Biff tried to make me eat something called Vegemate (at least that's what it sounded like). The stuff looked like puréed dog poop. I opted for a bowl of Wheety Snax and a juice. Call me boring, but I've never been a big fan of dog poop on toast.

"So," I said through a mouthful of crumbs, "what's the plan today?"

I was looking forward to seeing a bit of Shark Bay, maybe getting my toes wet (just my toes), and then taking a look at where I was supposed to be having my exhibition. Just thinking those words— *my exhibition*—gave me chills.

The first bit of bad news was that we wouldn't be going to the exhibition space just yet.

"They're still painting the place, Rafe," Biff said. "Should be finished by tomorrow."

Before I could say anything, Brad and Belinda dripped in from the pool, drying their cool surfie hair with cool surfie towels. Their eyes shot cool surfie daggers at me.

We exchanged nods, and Belinda leaned toward Brad and whispered something. Both of them looked back at me and started giggling. If you've ever had that happen to you, you'll know it feels about as reassuring as finding a bug in your burger.

Or a snake in your bed.

I could see that the Coogan kids and I were going to have an interesting relationship, and by "interesting" I mean I flat-out hated them.

"So," Mom said, "me and Mr. and Mrs. Coogan are going to walk to the lighthouse. It was built in 1882! It's the first example of reflected electric light in this part of Australia."

I tried to look impressed.

I failed.

"Great," I said.

Mom smiled. "I didn't think you'd go for that, so you're going with Brad and Belinda and all their friends to the beach! Won't that be great?"

I spat my Wheety Snax across the table. I'm sure if Brad and Belinda had been eating any they'd have done the same.

That was the second bit of bad news.

CHAPTER 20

THE SHORTS FROM HELL

Pretty much everyone in Shark Bay was drop-dead gorgeous.

Or maybe it was just the people who Brad and Belinda hung out with. Either way, ten minutes after leaving the Coogans' place I found myself heading for the beach with Brad and Belinda and a whole bunch of tall, fit, blond kids who looked like they fell right off a Tourism Australia ad. It was horrible.

"Pod people," Leo whispered, but I didn't reply because I didn't want the pod people thinking I was onto them. Besides, from painful personal experience, I've learned that it's embarrassing talking to yourself out loud.

To make matters worse (as if that was possible), my online fame had spread faster than the bubonic plague. In the ten minutes it took to walk to the beach, three kids recognized me from completefails.com. They shouted insults, none of which I can repeat.

Just as we reached Bloodspurt Beach (I'm not kidding, that's what it's called) we passed some kids sitting in the shade of a tree who looked like they were in the wrong movie. For a start, none of them was particularly tall, particularly fit, or particularly blond. They wore clothes that weren't surfie cool, they had hair that didn't look like anyone in Brad and Belinda's crew, and they all looked like they'd just sucked on a slice of lemon.

I liked them.

"Look at those sad sacks cluttering up the beach," Belinda said. "Total drongos."

I didn't know what a drongo was but it sounded bad. I was probably a drongo.

"The Outsiders," Brad said. He growled at one of the boys in the group, who jumped back nervously. Brad and his friends burst out laughing.

A dark-haired girl wearing black-rimmed glasses scowled at me.

I made a gesture that was meant to say, "Hey, sorry about all that, but I'm not really one of these cool surfie types at all. I'm more of an arty, interesting sort of guy and I'm sure we could be friends if you'd only give it a shot." But it's hard to get all that into one facial expression. I ended up looking like I was miming the best way to get the top off a coconut.

I blushed, and the girl in the glasses lowered the temperature of her already sub-zero stare before turning back to the rest of The Outsiders.

solid ice

As the Coogan twins and their entourage headed onto the sand, I fell back. I wanted to hang with The Outsiders. They seemed much cooler than Brad and Belinda's stupid buddies. They had a cool name, even if it wasn't one they had chosen for themselves. They looked like they might do some interesting stuff when they weren't hanging around the beach looking miserable. But from the expression on the dark-haired girl's face, it was clear that any friend of Brad and Belinda's was most definitely *not* a friend of theirs. They didn't like me.

Or my shorts.

I should explain the shorts. Remember how Aussie Airways lost our bags? That meant I had to borrow a pair of boardshorts from Brad. Mom had insisted, and Brad gave me these monstrosities. He must have been keeping them as a practical joke.

THE SHORTS FROM Hell..

For a start, they were about six sizes too big. More *longs* than shorts. They could have doubled as a tent. If the wind picked up to anything above a gentle breeze I'd have been hoisted into the air like an empty plastic bag. And they had the *nastiest* pattern ever produced by humans on them. They were covered in psychedelic day-glo butterflies, rainbows, hearts, and more pukey stuff like that. These shorts were so bright you could probably see them from space.

My pale Hills Valley winter legs hung from the bottom of them like a couple of straws.

I turned away from The Outsiders with a sigh and trudged after the pod people and toward Bloodspurt Beach.

CHAPTER 21

LET'S GO SURFING

Things went something like this:

1. Brad and his crew picked up their boards and headed for the water.

2. I didn't want to look like a bigger loser than I already was, so I said I'd love to go surfing but unfortunately I didn't have a surfboard. (See what I did there? This way, I could still look cool without actually having to go surfing.)

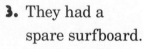
Hey, isn't that Snake-Fail Boy?

3. They had a spare surfboard.

4. I went surfing.

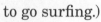

I tried to whip up some courage as we walked to the water's edge. I mean, I'd seen surfers surfing on TV. How hard could it be? I could swim and

I could skateboard, and surfing was really just skateboarding on water, right? I might even be really good at it, I thought.

And if I *was* really good at it, later on, Brad and Belinda and all the other cool surfie types would gather around the beach bonfire to hear me talk about taming The Big One. It might turn out to be the best thing I ever did!

One more time, Rafe! Tell us one more time, please!

It wasn't.

CHAPTER 22

A FREAKIN' HUGE SHARK

Attention! *This is a Rafe Khatchadorian Public Health Warning!*

Don't be like me. Don't listen to the voices in your head that tell you things will turn out okay. They won't. Above all, don't be dumb enough to go surfing. Trust me, it will end badly. Very badly.

This is because:

(a) surfing is VERY, VERY hard to do; and

(b) surfing absolutely *sucks*.

1. Surfing sucks so much that you could stick a hose on it and vacuum clean your house in six seconds flat.
2. Surfing sucks so much it could double as a black hole in space.
3. Surfing sucks the big patootie.
4. Surfing is the definition of suckosity.
5. And surfing in Australia is the suckiest of all because there are so many different ways to get maimed, injured, drowned, gouged, mocked, grazed, sliced, diced, and iced.

Listen and learn from my mistakes.

This is what surfing is really like.

In Hills Valley, where I live, the closest thing to a crystal-blue ocean is the public swimming pool, which isn't an ocean and is more of a slime-green color. Before I give you the nasty details on what happened out there, it is only fair to say that in Australia the ocean does look awesome.

That is pretty much the only fantastic thing about it. It looks good but, for some reason, the

Pacific Ocean took a dislike to me right from the start.

The first thing I noticed was that the waves were much bigger close up than they looked from the shore.

They are, in fact, ginormous.

The second problem is that getting the massive lump of plastic (aka the surfboard) past the breakers was almost impossible.

To make matters worse, the thing was strapped to my leg with a rope, which helped it snap back and smack into my head over and over again.

And by the time I did eventually scramble
my way past the crashing white foam, I was a
total wreck. I'd worked so hard to get to that
point that I swear my eyeballs were sweating.
My eyeballs! I didn't even know eyeballs *could*
sweat.

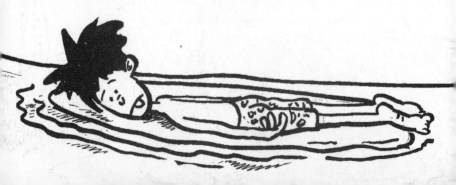

And all of those problems were accompanied by another, bigger fear—sharks.

The entire time I was getting knocked about by the waves and gulping down lungfuls of salt water, there was the constant terror that somewhere beneath was a FREAKIN' HUGE SHARK.

I swear I could hear the theme from *Jaws*. Whatever was down there would be so big that I'd be lifted up on a sort of bridge made of water as the FREAKIN' HUGE SHARK surfaced and I would get my first real look at the creature that was about to eat me.

It would throw me up in the air like it was tossing a marshmallow. At the top of my arc I would, just for a second, hang in the air above the beast—did I mention it was HUGE?—and see people on the beach running around like ants, screaming and panicking like you would if you'd just seen a FREAKIN' HUGE SHARK.

And then I'd be falling down, down, down, right into its gaping red maw.

Of course, since I'm still here, you'll have guessed that I didn't get eaten by a FREAKIN' HUGE SHARK. But surfing that morning on Bloodspurt Beach was, hands down, no contest, the worst hour of my life—worse than getting beat up by Miller the Killer. Worse than getting expelled. Worse than the worst thing you can think of times six. I almost drowned. I think I swallowed about 8 percent of the Pacific Ocean. It was like being trapped inside a giant washing machine set to SPIN. The ocean played with me for an hour and then spat me ashore like a gorilla spitting out an orange pip.

After all that, you'd think I'd be grateful to be back on dry land, and I would have been except

that when I did get back to the beach I was
unconscious.

As things turned out, *that* was the least of
my problems.

CHAPTER 23

THE NAKED TRUTH

Being shredded by a massive wave after
spending an hour in heavy surf and then
landing unconscious on an Australian beach is
not recommended. I would have died for sure
if it hadn't been for the dark-haired girl from
The Outsiders.

When my skinny surf-bashed body washed up
into the shallows (I found out later) she sprinted
across the sand, turned me over, and started giving
me the kiss of life.

That was when
I woke up and
thanked my
rescuer by
coughing a
lungful of
Pacific Ocean
all over her.

My name is Rafe and I am a pukeaholic. I haven't puked on anyone for three days.

What was it with us Khatchadorians? We just couldn't stop puking on Australians.

The dark-haired girl jumped to her feet, spattered with Khatchadorian lung drool. She turned on her heel and stalked back toward the trees, which was understandable.

I jumped to my feet. "Wait!" I yelled, or at least I would have if my lungs weren't filled with another 68 gallons of salt water. My voice sounded strange because my ears were full of water. I coughed up another bucketload and then ran after her. "Wait up!" I yelled.

I ran right through the busiest part of the beach and, as I ran, I began to notice a strange sound getting louder and louder. I ignored it and pursued my rescuer.

When the dark-haired girl reached the park, she glanced back and, spotting me, put her hand to her mouth in shock. At that same moment, the water blocking my ears was dislodged and sound rushed in.

The first thing I heard was laughter—lots of it. And a few screams.

I looked round. About eleventy billion Australians were standing up, pointing at me and laughing.

I mean, I know I wasn't the best surfer ever, but this reaction was a bit over the top. And my shorts weren't *that* ridiculous, were they? I glanced down at them to check for myself and realized instantly why the good people of Shark Bay were laughing.

My psychedelic, day-glo, see-them-from-space shorts had been ripped off in the surf. I was completely, absolutely, totally naked.

CHAPTER 24

CAN YOU GET RADIOACTIVE SHARKS ONLINE?

"You are proving very troublesome, Coogan."

I sat back in my white leather swivel chair ($952 from EvilGeniusFurniture.com) and stroked Mr. Barkley's fluffy white fur. Mr. Barkley purred softly.

"You have embarrassed me, and *that* I simply cannot allow." I pointed to the sharks in the pit. "Take a look at my little pets. They are very fine creatures, no? Their teeth have been specially sharpened by my assistant."

"Look," Brad whined, "whoever you are, I'm sorry!"

"My name is Rafe Khatchadorian, and you killed my father. Prepare to die!"

"I didn't kill your father!"

"No? Oh, wait, that's from something else," I said. I was getting mixed up. "But you are still going to die."

"Please, Dr. Khatchadorian," Brad begged. "I'm so, so sorry! It won't happen again, I swear!"

"Oh, you are right about that, Coogan." I smirked. "It will never happen again."

I leaned forward and pressed a button to release Coogan's chains.

"NOOOOOOOO!" Brad screamed as he disappeared below the boiling surface of the water.

"Mwahahaha!" I cackled. "Let that be a lesson to all enemies of Dr. Khatchadorian! Mwahahahaha!"

I would have made a great evil genius. No, really, I would have. Unfortunately I didn't have a secret lair or a pit of radioactive sharks.

Did I mention the sharks were radioactive?

A true evil genius never takes any chances. I didn't even have a cat, let alone a fluffy white one.

I would have to think of something else.

I was back at the Coogan place. A woman at Bloodspurt Beach had given me a towel and I had walked back through the laughing crowds, my face as red as a Mars sunset.

It had been the longest walk of my life. After getting cleaned up and dressed I sat by the Coogans' pool in the shade of a pandanus tree and thought dark, dark thoughts of vengeance.

Brad Coogan would pay. Mark my words.

CHAPTER 25

KELL-ING ME SOFTLY

I came up blank on ideas for Brad's payback. After almost two hours of sulking by the pool, all I had to show for my efforts was a sunburned neck and a fat white splat of lorikeet poop on my shoulder. I didn't even wipe off the poop—that's how miserable I was.

Around 3 pm I heard a car pull up outside, and a few minutes later, Mom came onto the pool deck with Biff and Barb Coogan and a tall tanned man wearing a khaki shirt, mirrored sunglasses, and shorts that were a little *too* short.

Short-shorts guy and Mom were laughing about something. Instantly, my super-spidey senses went into overdrive.

"Hi, Rafe," Mom sang. She looked happy.

I didn't like it.

I mean, I want my mom to be happy and everything, but there was something about short-shorts guy that put me on alert.

"Did you have a good time at the beach?" Mom asked.

"Of course he did!" short shorts said before I could reply. "Who wouldn't have a good time on a ripper of a day like this? Catch any waves, grommet?"

He bent down and (I swear this is true) *ruffled my hair*. My hair hadn't been ruffled since I was in kindergarten, and I hadn't liked it much back then.

Ruffle

"Oh, it was great," I said. "Apart from Brad trying to drown me, and me ending up naked in the middle of the beach."

"Oh dear," Mom said, suddenly concerned. "That must have been awful, Rafe."

"That's right," short shorts said. "Awfully funny!"

"I can't see why," I said, in as frosty a voice as I could manage.

"No need to get your undies in a knot, mate," short shorts said. "You need to lighten up a bit. Take that frown and put it upside down!"

I was beginning to rethink my attitude about feeding someone to radioactive sharks.

"This is Kell," Mom said. "He's a friend of Biff and Barb's. Kell's a geologist who works for a big mining company."

I shrugged.

"Be nice, Rafey," she said, giving me a look. "I'll let you two talk." Mom headed back into the house with Biff and Barb.

Kell put out a hand the size of a bulldozer scoop. I could see myself reflected back in his shades. "Kell Weathers," he said. "Pleased to meet you, little man."

I let that "little man" bit slide and put my hand out reluctantly. "Rafe."

Kell gripped my hand and shook. I might as well have shoved my hand into a garbage disposal.

There'll be more on Kell later.

Much more.

CHAPTER 26

THE ARTIST
HAS LANDED

I didn't see much of the twins over the next couple of days, which was just fine by me. Belinda did snarkily mention about two hundred times that my "CompleteFails" clip was up to 387,765 hits or whatever, and Brad put salt on my Wheety Snax, but other than that they left me to do my own thing.

One of which was going with Biff and Mom to see the Shark Bay Surf Club, where the artwork I was supposed to be making—the whole point of this trip and something that I'd almost forgotten about—was going to be exhibited.

My artwork, whatever that turned out to be, whenever I got around to actually producing any,

was going to take pride of place in the foyer of
the new club.

"Not bad, hey?" Biff said.

I had to admit it was pretty cool. Actually, the
place was much cooler than I had imagined.

"Your painting will be center stage, Rafe," Biff said. "Just to the left of the waterfall."

Mom beamed. "It's going to be fantastic!"

"I haven't done anything yet," I said.

Mom put her arm around my shoulders. "Whatever you do will be fantastic, honey."

"You'll be a knockout," Biff said. "We're all looking forward to seeing the great artist's work!"

No pressure then. I gulped and wandered around the lobby, trying to look like I knew what I was doing.

The waterfall was right at the entrance to the new surf club. A cascade of water poured down a fake rock wall into a great big pool. There were blue and green lights under the water, which made the whole thing shimmer. It looked amazing. I couldn't imagine *anything* I produced standing a chance if it was anywhere near this.

Gulp!

I took some photos of the place. I didn't have a clue what I was going to do, but I hoped the photos would give me some ideas.

The only unfinished thing about the club was that the toilets weren't working yet. I saw a row of grey boxes outside lined up on the small lawn to one side of the surf club entrance.

"Temporary dunnies," Biff said. He explained that a "dunny" was Australian for "toilet".

Biff had also come up with a place for me to work in—a big, well-stocked room at the Shark Bay College. The place had everything I could possibly need to make something special, which, considering I had ABSOLUTELY NO IDEA about what to fill the exhibition space with, made me even more nervous than I already was.

CHAPTER 27

THE OUTSIDERS

After a couple of days without anything very interesting happening, I decided to skate down to the college and see if I could stare at some blank pieces of paper down there. I grabbed Brad's best board from his room—one he'd told me never to touch—and headed out.

Rounding the bend coming down the hill to Bloodspurt Beach, I smacked straight into another skater. It was the dark-haired girl from the beach. I braced myself for some sort of insult about how lame I was.

"Oh, you," she said. "The artist."

I blinked. Me? And then I realized I *was* the artist. "How do you know who I am?" I asked.

The girl got to her feet. "Are you kidding? Everyone in town is talking about the crazy American nudist artist who has his own CompleteFails clip." She stuck out her hand. "Ellie's the name."

We shook hands and, for once, Rafe Khatchadorian managed to say the right thing to a girl.

"Would you like a smoothie?" I asked. It wasn't the best line ever but she said yes, so I must have done something right.

The usual Khatchadorian girl conversation style

There's a first time for everything.

We skated across to the T-Rex burger joint, where the dinosaur had been put back in his rightful place. He looked happy to be there again.

"On me," I said, pushing Ellie's mango smoothie across the table when it arrived. "For saving my life."

I don't know what was smoother, me or what was in the glass.

Ellie put a finger in her mouth and mimed puking. "Puh-lease," she said. "Can't you see I'm eating? Or drinking. Do you eat or drink a smoothie?"

Rex's MighteeBites

I wasn't too sure but we carried on talking for a while. Ellie told me all about growing up right here in Shark Bay and how she'd always felt like she didn't belong. The rest of her friends were kind of the same, which is how they ended up hanging out together.

I admit I was a little jealous. I wished I had my own group of misfits back home. All I had was Leo.

"You know," Ellie said, "I thought you were one of the Coogan bozos when I saw you heading out into the surf."

I shook my head. "Just visiting. I had no idea what I was doing."

"The Coogans should have known better," Ellie said. "It's *dangerous* out in the surf." She paused and looked straight into my soul with her special truth-seeking laser-beam eyes. (Did I mention she had eyes like lasers? No? Well, she does.) "Unless you were dumb enough to *pretend* you could surf?"

"Um." I looked down at the table. My voice got real small. "I might have, sort of, kinda said I could . . ."

Ellie shook her head. "I thought so. Even the Coogans wouldn't send a newbie out there. And for them the surf's not such a big deal. They like to think of themselves as the bravest family in town. Nothing scares Brad Coogan—except frogs. He was in my biology class at school and kind of freaked out when a frog got loose."

"Frogs, hey?" I said.

You know this is going to feature later, right?

And I thought the toilet-block thing was going too far. Now it's frogs?

A tickle of a whisper of a possibility popped into my mind, but I decided to leave it for now. The Big Revenge Plan could wait. I was enjoying myself for just about the first time since I'd arrived in Australia.

I took a slurp of my smoothie. "Your friends and that bunch don't get along?"

Ellie nodded. "You could say that. Brad and the other morons dubbed us The Outsiders, thinking it was an insult, but we kind of liked it, so that's what we call ourselves. And we're into different things to them. That beach stuff isn't really our idea of fun. I mean, a couple of the guys surf, but it's not our thing."

"So what is your thing?" I asked.

"Movies," Ellie said, her eyes lighting up. "We make horror movies."

I hadn't seen that one coming, but as soon as Ellie said the words, I had a real lightbulb moment. I leaned closer. "Tell me more."

CHAPTER 28

A DROP BEAR ATE MY SANGA

I looked at Kell Weathers dangling helplessly at the end of my arm. He'd made the mistake of trying his old hand-crushing handshake routine once too often.

What Weathers hadn't reckoned with was that I'd signed up as a NASA test subject for an experimental android technology.

"Would you like a sausage sandwich?" Robo-Kell Scorpion said.

Considering the situation, it seemed like a funny thing to say.

"Rafe?" Robo-Kell said again. "Sausage sandwich? Drink?"

I blinked and saw Mom looking at me strangely. There was no sign of Robo-Kell Scorpion. I had fallen asleep on a sunlounger next to the barbecue grill on the Coogans' pool deck in the middle of the party.

"What?" I said.

"You were miles away," Mom said. She put her hand across my forehead in the way that moms do.

"I wish I was miles away," I mumbled.

"Play nice," Mom said. "For me?"

I sighed and nodded.

Mom was right. She was enjoying her holiday in Australia and I didn't want to spoil things for her, even if she did have a blind spot when it came to Australian geologists. The sky was blue and the sun was shining. What did I have to complain about?

Especially since I was meeting Ellie and the rest of The Outsiders at the movies later. With *that* to look forward to I could manage the next few hours. Although, as Mom wandered toward where Kell Weathers was talking to Biff, I felt the fingers of my right hand twitch. A steel robotic claw would come in handy sometimes.

I stretched, yawned, then got up to go do my
Mom-pleasing duty. The place was packed with the
great and the good (and not-so-good) of Shark Bay.
As Mom reached Kell, he looked in my direction
and smiled. I got that super-spidey tingle all over
again. I'd have to watch this situation closely.

The party wasn't as bad as I'd thought it would
be. At one point Biff dragged me around like some
sort of trophy and introduced me as "the American
artist." Surprisingly, people seemed interested, so I

relaxed and tried to enjoy the experience. But after an hour of smiling so much my jaw ached, I grabbed some food and my sketchbook and found a quiet spot under the trees by the pool. I had just taken a bite of my cheese sandwich and started drawing when Kell appeared, holding a can of soda.

"Thought you looked a bit thirsty there, Rafey," he said, passing me the can. The soda was ice-cold.

I looked at it suspiciously.

"Look," Kell continued, "I know we haven't exactly hit it off, but I'm not really a bad guy and I couldn't let you stand around over here without giving you a heads-up, you being from overseas and everything."

"A heads-up?"

Kell pointed at the branches above my head. "It's highly unlikely, but we do have a small problem in Australia: Drop bears. You heard of 'em?"

A chill ran down my back.

Drop bear

"There are drop bears here?" I said, looking up at the trees.

Kell nodded. "They know when there's fresh meat in the neighborhood." He eyed my sandwich. "And they do love a cheese sanga. Watch yourself, mate."

I looked at Kell. Maybe I'd been wrong about him. Perhaps he wasn't so bad after all.

"Thanks," I said, and opened the can.

As I did, two things happened.

The first was that the soda exploded all over my face, temporarily blinding me.

The second (and this one was much more worrying) was that I felt something furry fall onto my head and wrap its arms around my neck.

A drop bear!

I screamed like a startled pony and leapt backwards. For a split second, my feet teetered on the edge of the pool and then, with an almighty splash, I fell in head first, clawing wildly at the drop bear. I wasted no time in expertly sucking in about 83 gallons of chlorinated water and sank below the surface, sure that at any moment the thing was going to rip open the top of my skull

Aussie Food Explained

sandwich = **Sanga**

sausage = **Snag**

candy = **lollies**

Moreton Bay Bug = **Revolting Space Alien**

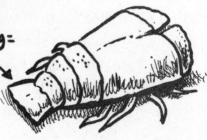

and commence drop-bear dinner. Main course:
Khatchadorian Brain à la mode.

I erupted from the surface of the pool like a
ballistic missile leaving a submarine, dragging the
creature off my neck. Without hanging around to

see what had happened to the drop bear, I kicked toward the edge of the pool so fast I felt as though someone had strapped an outboard motor onto my rear end and pressed the START button.

Through a foam of white water (caused by my high-speed flailing arms), I wondered why no one was diving in to save me. Couldn't they see that I was about to be eaten alive? Or maybe they were too scared of the drop bear? And then I saw the pool was surrounded by laughing faces.

I stopped swimming and looked around. A soft toy bobbed on the surface of the pool. I looked up and glimpsed Brad in the branches of a nearby tree, laughing like he'd just swallowed a joke book.

The whole dirty trick became as clear as the Coogans' swimming pool.

I'd been had. In public. Again.

I clambered out of the pool with as much dignity as I could. Which, in case you were wondering, was exactly zero.

"C'mon, Rafey," Kell shouted as I stalked toward the house. "It's only a joke, mate!"

I said nothing, but one thing was certain. Kell Weathers had just joined Brad Coogan at the very, very top of the Rafe Khatchadorian Revenge List.

CHAPTER 29

YOU WON'T LIKE ME
WHEN I'M ANGRY

It was horrible.

Eyes like oysters, gaping mouth full of tombstone teeth, flaking, clammy skin. I felt my breathing becoming panicky as the thing reached out toward me, its bony hands getting closer and closer and . . .

I whipped off my 3D glasses and sank back into my seat as the zombies swam out of focus. I risked a quick glance at Ellie to see if she'd noticed the big fat yellow streak running down my back.

She had.

"Are you okay?" she whispered.

I rubbed the bridge of my nose. "Um, these glasses give me a headache."

"Uh-huh." Ellie's smile made me suspect she might not have believed me, but she returned her gaze to the screen without saying anything else.

I left the glasses off and watched the rest of *Zombies Ate My Brain* in a happy red-and-green haze. Just before the movie ended I put the 3D glasses back on so the rest of The Outsiders wouldn't think I was a total wimp.

We slurped on slurpees in the movie theatre cafe and discussed the finer points of zombie etiquette. Now would probably be a good time to properly introduce The Outsiders. If this was a superhero comic I'd tell you all about their special skills, but they were just a bunch of kids. And that was okay by me.

Dingbat Ellie Mikey Sal Nico

The Outsiders knew *a lot* about zombies.

They knew a lot about horror movies of every description, period. I was impressed and got a whole lot more impressed when I found out that Ellie was The Outsider in charge of special effects.

"She's good," Nico said. "Ellie knows her stuff, bro."

The rest of The Outsiders nodded.

"You should see her latest," Nico said. "It's a beaut."

"It's a bunyip," Sal added. She was the smallest of The Outsiders and was almost hidden behind her slurpee.

"A what?" I said.

"*Revenge of the Teenage Zombie Bunyip From Mars*," Ellie said. "That's our new movie. Bunyips are these weird sort of giant amphibians."

"I've never heard of them," I said.

"They're pretty much strictly an Aussie thing," Ellie said. She sounded sort of proud. "Like frogs, but bigger and angrier."

My ears pricked up at the mention of frogs and—BING!—just like that, a magnificently evil plan began to form in my brain. A plan for revenge. A plan so monstrous that it would probably lead to the collapse of civilization—or the part of civilization that included Shark Bay.

The only question was, would I risk everything to get even with Brad?

I was still thinking about that when Ellie took me to one side.

"What's up?" I said.

She frowned. "You haven't seen it?"

BUNYIP

"Seen what?"

Ellie held out her phone and pressed the PLAY button on a video clip. It was only a short piece of footage—me doing the whole screaming-and-falling-into-the-Coogan-pool thing. The clip had racked up eleventy trillion hits already. I hadn't mentioned the drop bear incident to Ellie.

I played it cool. If you can call turning the color of a stoplight cool. What's that? No, you can't? Okay, I *didn't* play it cool. I was mad. I was *seething*.

"Are you all right?" Ellie asked.

"NYAAAAARGGGH!" I roared as I started to swell up and turn green right there in the middle of the cafe. My eyes glowed fiery red and muscles I didn't know I had bulged from my arms. I ripped open my shirt, flexed my giant green biceps, and roared like a wounded lion. I lifted a fist the size of a basketball and smashed a life-sized cut-out of Leonardo DiCaprio into smithereens. As people started screaming and running in all directions I stamped a big green foot. The ground shook. I—

"Rafe!" Ellie said. "I said, are you all right?"

I blinked and looked down at my skinny
non-green arm. "Sorry, I was miles away." I laced
my fingers together and cracked my knuckles.
"This bunyip of yours," I said to Ellie, "can I see it?"

CHAPTER 30

SELFISH? ME?

The next day I had to wait for Ellie to get home from school before I could go and see the bunyip.

The hours crawled past. The Coogans were out at work and Mom had gone off somewhere with my archenemy, Kell Weathers. What with Brad and Belinda and Kell, not to mention the rest of The Surf Gorillas, that list of sworn enemies was getting longer than one of Grandma Dotty's shopping lists. And that's without bringing up all the sworn enemies I have back in America.

Of all my sworn enemies, Kell was the one who worried me most. I wanted revenge on Brad, but Kell's friendship with Mom was a teeny-tiny concern.

Leo, who had been keeping a low profile recently, popped up and passed me a drawing.

"Very funny," I said. But maybe Leo was right. Perhaps I *was* being shellfish—I mean selfish. Maybe Mom *deserved* some attention, even if it was from a hand-crushing creep like Kell.

Reluctantly, I crossed Weathers off my list of enemies. We'd never be what you might call buddies, but I didn't need to let my dislike of KW spoil Mom's trip. I felt a warm glow inside, and it wasn't because I'd accidentally swallowed a chili. I felt *noble*.

When it was time for me and my halo to go to Ellie's place, I grabbed Brad's prized skateboard and zipped there as fast as I could go.

It had been a hot day and the thunderclouds had been building for hours. As I reached Ellie's street, the first fat raindrops began to fall and I heard the distant rumble of thunder.

Ellie lived a few blocks back from the beach in a less swanky part of Shark Bay, where the houses were made of timber and stood on stilts. Lots of them had small boats in the yard or old cars that were being fixed up. The streets were lined with shady trees and the whole place was a lot funkier than down by the shore. It felt more like where I came from. I liked it.

I hoped this bunyip of Ellie's matched my vision of it. I walked up to her door and knocked. My whole plan depended on Ellie's bunyip.

No pressure.

CHAPTER 31

I WAS WORKING IN THE LAB LATE ONE NIGHT . . .

"Hi," Ellie said when she opened the door.

"I'm here," I announced, smiling.

"I can see that, Einstein," Ellie said.

She had a point.

"And stop smiling like that. It makes you look like a nut." She turned and walked back into the house. "Follow me. My dad's still at work."

I almost asked where her mom was when I remembered Nico mentioning that Ellie's mom had died when she was little. That would have been great,

Khatchadorian, I said to myself. Real tactful.
I reached up and adjusted my imaginary halo.

Ellie's house was just like a regular house—
not too tidy, TV, kitchen, furniture. A bit boring,
really. But downstairs, things were different.
Very different.

"My dad put in walls between the stilts to make
this into a basement," Ellie explained. "It might be
a problem if the place ever gets flooded again, but
we'll deal with that when it happens. Until then,
this is my workshop!"

I couldn't speak. Ellie's workshop was the
coolest place I'd ever seen. The walls were lined
with shelves of paint, tools, boxes, bits of models,
plastic horror masks, electronics, lights, rolls
of canvas, paper, lengths of wood, coils of wire,
aerosol spraycans, cleaning fluids, remote-
controlled devices, mirrors—anything that
looked like it might be useful when making an
animatronic bunyip was there.

A massive, paint-spattered wooden workbench
stretched the length of Ellie's workshop. Lying in
the centre of another workbench was something
under a dust sheet. A spaghetti mess of wires

snaked out from whatever was there and dripped onto the floor of the basement. A vice at one end of the bench was holding what looked like an alien arm.

Ellie pulled back the sheet. "There he is."

Thunder cracked outside, and lightning cast shadows which flickered across the walls. Lying flat on its back, missing an arm, and looking exactly like it was asleep, was Ellie's bunyip.

It was *gigantic*.

It was *terrifying*.

It was **perfect**.

"Wow," I said.

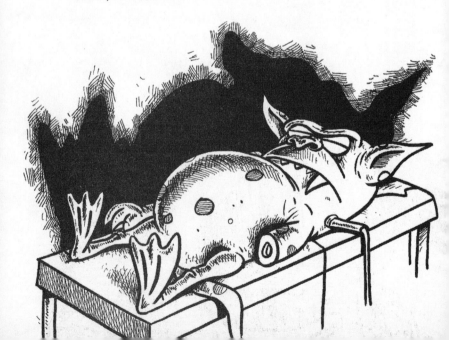

As reactions go it wasn't the best I'd ever heard, but it was from the heart. The bunyip was *wow*. It was as *wow* as anything I could remember ever seeing. It frightened *me* half to death and I knew it was just a bundle of rubber and electronics.

"That is amazing. Does it move?" I asked.

Ellie picked up a remote control from the workbench and pressed a switch. There was a soft electronic hum and then the bunyip's eyes glowed red. Ellie turned a dial on the remote and the bunyip sat up on the bench. It swung its head in my direction and howled so loudly I could feel the bass shaking my spine.

"One hundred and forty-three decibels," Ellie said proudly. "Twin-mounted deep-bass equalized

speakers with double woofers and a Swiss-made magnifying reverberator."

I didn't understand a word she'd said but I knew one thing: I was in love (with Ellie's bunyip, in case you were wondering).

"I've got a plan," I said. I didn't mean to say anything, but seeing the bunyip made the words just come rushing out. *Ivegotaplan.* Blurp! Just like that.

"What for?" Ellie said.

I shook my head. "Forget I said anything."

Ellie tilted her head to one side and looked at me, her lips pursed. "Is this about getting revenge on Brad and Belinda?"

I don't know if Ellie was some sort of mind-reader or what—for all I knew she could be a star graduate from the Zurich Institute of Mind-Meld—but she had read *my* thoughts as clearly as a billboard.

"Is it that obvious?"

Ellie nodded.

"So . . .?"

Ellie didn't say anything for about a hundred years.

"I'll think about it," she said eventually. "I have to live here once you go back to Hell Valley. And I'm guessing this plan might involve my bunyip, right? I put a lot of work into that."

I nodded. I didn't correct her about Hills Valley. It didn't seem important. What did seem important was that Ellie was contemplating helping me out with my plan.

It was a start.

CHAPTER 32

THE PLAN: DAY ONE

My mission, should I choose to accept it—and I had choosened—was to get into the Shark Bay Surf Club, take measurements, and get out, all while staying alive, if possible.

I braced myself against the edge of the skylight, hooked the titanium wire onto my belt, and adjusted my night-vision goggles. Below me, the raging torrent of the waterfall rushed past before falling almost six thousand miles to the boiling pool set into the floor of the lobby far, far below.

"Careful, Khatchadorian," Ivan Awfulich, my Mission Controller, snarled as I leaned out into empty space. "You've only got one shot at this! If you mess up, HQ are going to bury you so deep they'll need a team of miners to find you."

"Check," I said.

I had my analogue-level measuring device (a tape measure) in one hand and a state-of-the-art measurement-recording platform (a notebook) in the other. My image-retention device (a camera) was hanging around my neck.

I gave Ivan a final salute and dropped into the abyss, heading for the lobby at the end of the wire, my face only inches from the waterfall. One slip and I could get seriously splashed.

Down, down, down I slid until I reached a point just above the surface of the pool and stopped dead, perfectly balanced only inches from the water. The night-vision goggles identified the tracks of the surf club's security-system lasers and . . . that's what I would have done if I couldn't get in any other way. In the end, I just walked up and went inside. See why I had to spice it up a little?

The lobby of the club was deserted, apart from a woman who looked like she might be the manager—and that's exactly who she was.

"Take your time, darl," the manager said. She pointed at a poster on the wall. "Have you sorted out your costume yet?"

"Costume?" I said.

The poster was advertising the grand opening. My name was up there and I experienced a little thrill seeing my name in print.

"Nobody mentioned fancy dress," I said, but the manager had gone off to do whatever it is managers do.

I hadn't considered the possibility that this thing would have fancy-dress requirements. Fancy dress seemed to figure a lot in Australia. Biff had

SHARK BAY SURF CLUB
GRAND OPENING
JOIN US FOR A NIGHT OF FUN AS WE CELEBRATE THE BRAND NEW SBSC!
FEATURING THE WORK OF ARTIST RAFE KHATCHADORIAN!
TICKETS $10 FROM RECEPTION.
FANCY DRESS REQUIRED!

picked us up at the airport dressed as a chicken after all. I guessed fancy dress was another one of those mysterious Australian things, like cricket and Vegemite and wearing short shorts. It was also a complication I could do without, but then, as I considered it more carefully, I realized that the fancy dress could come in handy.

I opened up my measurement-recording platform, unrolled my analogue-level measuring device, and started taking measurements. If we were going to get this right we couldn't afford making a single mistake.

CHAPTER 33

ACTION!

I'd never been on a film set before.

To be honest, it wasn't as glamorous as I thought it would be, even allowing for the fact that it was just The Outsiders filming *Revenge of the Teenage Zombie Bunyip From Mars*.

We were standing around on a patch of scrubby ground next to a sugar cane field a couple of miles west of Shark Bay. The equipment they were using wasn't exactly hi-tech, but they seemed to know what they were doing.

The Outsiders were shooting on anything they could get—camcorders, smartphones, even an old Super-8 film camera that used actual film.

"We do most of the sound later," Nico explained. "There's usually too much background interference if we record it live."

They were filming a chase scene through the cane field and were having some trouble deciding how to do it. I tried to explain how it might be done by sketching out a few ideas, and that seemed to work.

"Hey! You can be our storyboard artist," Ellie said.

Until then I didn't know there was such a thing as a storyboard artist. I'd never thought about my drawings being *useful* before.

My storyboard →

① Cane field— misty... spooky

② Close up on Dingbat. Scared. Lost...

③ Dingbat's view: a "wall" of sugarcane.

④ Dingbat hears a sudden noise! Close-up.

⑤ Top of the sugar cane field. It's moving!

⑥ Dingbat runs!

I sat in the shade of a tree and started sketching. Maybe these drawings could become the exhibit at the surf club, I thought. I did need *something* there to deflect attention from my evil plan.

Everything was in place. Now all I had to do was convince Ellie and the gang to help. They were no fans of Brad and Belinda and the rest of The Surf Gorillas, but what I was planning needed some real motivation. The Outsiders hadn't been publicly humiliated like me.

As I sketched I wondered if they would risk everything just to help me get revenge.

CHAPTER 34

EGGSTERMINATE!

The push that sent Ellie over the edge came sooner than I'd thought.

It was the last shot of the day and the most complicated. It was also the most expensive by a long way. Ellie and the rest of The Outsiders had saved up a whole bunch of money for this shot and had bought some flash-bangs from a movie-prop

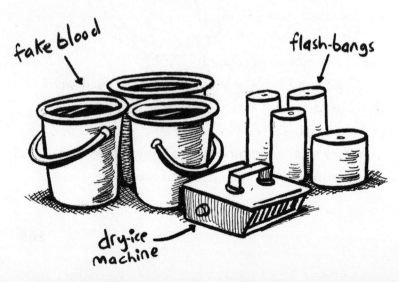

fake blood

flash-bangs

dry-ice machine

supplier in Sydney, hired a dry-ice machine from somewhere and had prepared buckets of fake blood.

"This has got to go right first time," Ellie said.

Nico, the director, gave instructions to Mikey and Dingbat, who were playing the two characters. It was down to Ellie to time the flash-bangs, set off the dry ice and throw the blood. Nico had one camera—the best one—and I was given a smartphone to film things from another angle, just as a backup. A third camcorder was propped up on a tree stump to film it as a long shot.

"Everyone ready?" Nico said. "Let's get this right, okay? We've got about three minutes of sunlight left!"

Ellie counted down the scene. "Three, two, one . . ."

"Action!" Nico yelled.

Ellie pressed the START button on the dry-ice machine, and we all began filming.

Mikey and Dingbat came out of the cane field right on cue, and Ellie started setting off the flash-bangs. They looked amazing. Ellie smiled and looked over at me. Grinning, I gave her the thumbs-up.

As Ellie threw the first of the buckets of fake blood over Dingbat, an egg exploded on the ground in front of her. She looked at it, puzzled, and then a second egg hit Mikey on the shoulder, followed by a bag of flour.

A shower of eggs and flour cascaded down on the set, and then crashing through the canes came The Surf Gorillas, yelling and screaming. Before any of The Outsiders could react, they ran through the set, scattering script sheets to the wind and kicking over the buckets of blood.

"Losers!" Brad shouted as they ran off laughing and hooting.

"Film this, you geeks!" Belinda screeched.

The Outsiders stood and watched them go.

The shot was ruined.

As the sky darkened, Ellie walked over to me. She had egg in her hair and an expression on her face that would not have looked out of place in a horror movie.

"This revenge plan of yours?" she said. "What do you need? I'm in."

CHAPTER 35

KELL GOES BARKING MAD

Life carried on as usual at the Coogans', which meant that Brad and Belinda took every opportunity to rub my nose in what a loser I was.

I didn't care. Much.

Let them think they'd gotten away with the Great Cane Field Ambush. Let them think I was too much of a wuss to get my own back. They'd find out soon enough that Rafe Khatchadorian was a force to be reckoned with.

A force to be reckoned with

Really?

As would Kell Weathers.

Kell had let his true nature slip again one evening when he came round to pick up my mom. She was busy getting ready upstairs when Kell took me over to a quiet corner after. (I'd been giving him the complete frost the last couple of times I'd seen him. I still remembered his part in the Great Drop Bear Incident and, even though I wasn't going to try to get revenge on him, I wasn't ready to let bygones be bygones either. It seemed that neither was Kell.)

"You don't like me too much, do you, *Rafe*?" He prodded me in the chest. It hurt. I guess geologists have strong fingers from picking up all those rocks.

I shrugged, trying to ignore the pain. Then Kell jabbed me again. It hurt again.

"I asked you a question, *Rafey*."

I shrugged once more and, right in front of my eyes, Kell began to mutate into a werewolf.

special werewolf shorts?

Hair sprouted from his face, and his hands curled into vicious-looking claws. His eyes glowed red and drool dripped from between fangs that slid down over his bottom lip. He looked a bit like Hugh Jackman's less-handsome Wolverine brother crossed with a German shepherd. The dog, I mean, not an actual shepherd from Germany.

"If I didn't like your mom so much I'd clobber you myself," Kell the Werewolf hissed.

I didn't even know werewolves *could* hiss, which just goes to show you learn something new every day.

"After tonight, you might not have anything to say about it. And if you mention a word of this to her I'll deny it all." Kell threw back his head and howled at the moon. There wasn't a moon visible so he howled at the lightbulb hanging from the ceiling. I guess werewolves can't always get full-moon access.

By the time Mom came downstairs looking glitzy, Kell had lost all trace of his inner werewolf. They're sneaky like that. Werewolves, I mean, not Australian geologists. Most Australian geologists are probably fine examples of human beings, but Kell wasn't doing their reputation any favors with me. As far as I was concerned, there was at least one too many Australian geologists stinking up the joint.

"Nice to see you two getting along," Mom said. She smiled so wide I didn't have the heart to tell her that her friend Kell was a chest-prodding bully. Plus a mutant werewolf.

"Best of mates," Kell said. He looked at me. "Isn't that right, Rafey?"

I nodded, not trusting myself to speak.

Mom and Kell headed out toward the bright lights of Shark Bay, laughing and joking like two lovebirds. Seeing Mom all dressed up, a horrible thought struck me: Kell Weathers is going to pop THE question tonight!

No one wants a werewolf as a stepfather. It wasn't so much him being a drooling creature of the night that worried me, although that would be

pretty inconvenient. It was him getting friendly with my mom. The night before, I'd used her laptop for something and had noticed she'd been reading up on Australia's immigration laws.

I had no real problem with Australians (other than Brad, Belinda, and The Surf Gorillas—and Kell, of course), but I'm not anxious to become one anytime soon. The whole thing was starting to make me depressed.

I went to my room, rubbing the sore spot on my chest, and sat down on the bed. This was going to require some thinking about.

CHAPTER 36

TRUE GRIT

When Mom and Kell got back from their night out, Kell grabbed me "playfully" around the neck and began ruffling my hair.

I hate having my hair ruffled by someone I *like*. Having it done by a creep like Kell Weathers almost made me hurl.

"Ow!" I yelled, rubbing my scalp.

Mom sighed. "Kell's just being nice, Rafe."

"Don't blame the little feller, Jules," Kell said. "The kid just needs some grit."

"Oh, you want grit?" I yelled. "I'll give you grit!"

I leapt across the room, grabbed Kell around the neck and threw him at the wall.

"Don't hurt me!" Kell squealed as he lay sprawled on the canvas.

"Rafe, stop!" Mom
yelled. "He's only a
geologist!"

"Too late!" I shouted.
"Rafe the Chafe takes no prisoners!"

I leapt from the top rope of the
ring and slammed into Kell, hard.
Wrapping my sandpapery legs
around his head, I began to chafe like no one has
ever chafed before. A grown man in the audience
burst into tears. Sandpapering a man's head is just

Oh, that's gotta hurt! Rafe "The Chafe" Khatchadorian looks like he's in a really scratchy mood tonight, folks!

CHAFE! CHAFE!

nasty, but I had been pushed to the limit, and I chafed even harder.

"Oh, the humanity!" the commentator wailed. "Won't the referee stop this madness? No one can take this kind of punishment! The Geologist won't have a head left if this goes on much longer!"

He was right. Within a minute all that remained of Kell's head was a pile of wood shavings.

I got to my feet and the referee lifted my arm in the air.

"And the winner is . . . Rafe! Rafe. Rafe. *RAFE?*"

I opened my eyes. Kell, his head far too intact for my liking, was leaning over me, my mom looking over his shoulder.

"You must have drifted off there for a minute, mate," Kell said. Then, with his back to my mom, he mouthed, "Wimp."

Kell Weathers was moving up the People Rafe Khatchadorian Hates chart fast.

If Brad Coogan wasn't around, he'd be number one, no sweat.

CHAPTER 37

LET'S GET THINGS STARTED

The next day, Ellie and I really got moving on Operation R.O.C.K. (Revenge on the Coogan Kids). With less than twenty-four hours to go before the big night at the surf club, there wasn't a moment to waste.

Ellie built a scale model of the surf club lobby out of cardboard and we plotted every step in miniature with the rest of The Outsiders.

"This thing's got to be perfect," I said, pacing the floor of Ellie's workshop. I pointed my pointy stick (everyone planning something like this needs a pointy stick) at the model. "And top secret. If word gets out to The Surf Gorillas, we're finished."

The Outsiders nodded solemnly. No one was going to snitch.

Nico and I went out to the club and cased the joint for the best time to get everything inside. We'd had a stroke of luck with our plans—it turned out Nico's older sister was the club manager.

"She keeps the key to it in her purse," Nico said as we crouched in the bushes across the road from the club.

"Can you get a copy?" I asked.

Nico held up a key and smiled. "Way ahead of you, dude."

"Tonight?"

Nico nodded. "Tonight."

Operation R.O.C.K. was a go.

CHAPTER 38

THE POINT
OF NO RETURN

It was The Big Night. We had done all we could.
Everything was in place.

The sketches I'd done for The Outsiders' shoot
had been framed and placed on three easels on a
small stage at one side of the waterfall. I'd called
the drawings "Zombie Movie Sketches" because,

well, they were sketches of the making of a zombie movie. I'm clever like that. Biff had put the title up in a big banner hung over the easels. It made me feel pretty special.

Last night the rest of The Outsiders and I had broken about nineteen billion laws and set up what we needed inside the surf club. We hadn't got much sleep, but we didn't care.

Tonight was payback time.

Ellie and I—she was dressed as Frankenstein's monster and I went as Igor—arrived around seven. As we neared the entrance, I could see through the windows that the place was already knee-deep in pirates and princesses, Elvises and Ewoks, highwaymen, aliens, ballerinas, boxers, and Batmen.

Brad, showing about as much imagination as a jellyfish in a coma, had gone as a 1970s surfer and Belinda was a punk rocker. Kell was a werewolf— spooky, right?—and my mom had gone as some kind of superhero.

Just outside the entrance a gorilla was cooking sausages on a giant grill. As Ellie and I walked by, the gorilla removed his head to reveal a sweating

Mayor Coogan, who looked like he was beginning
to regret his choice of fancy dress. Perhaps he
should have stuck with the chicken, puke-stink
and all.

"The star of the show!" Biff said
as he saw me. He waved a plate
of sausage sandwiches
at us. "Sausage sanga,
Picasso?"

I felt my stomach lurch and shook my head. I was so nervous that I was sure anything I ate would come straight back up. "No, thanks," I said, and darted inside.

Before I knew what was happening, Mom grabbed me and pulled me toward a man dressed all in black with a grey beard. "This is Frost DeAndrews, the famous art critic," she said. "He's come up all the way from Sydney!"

"Hi," I said. "What have you come as?"

DeAndrews looked puzzled, then pursed his lips. "We don't *do* fancy dress in Sydney."

Frost
DeAndrews

How to spot
an art critic...

Sunken eyes

Hipster beard

Lemon-sucking
lips

Black jacket

Heart of
solid ice
(not shown)

Hands in pockets
to indicate
total boredom
with EVERYTHING

Black jeans

General air of
superiority

Uncomfortable
shoes

"Oh," I said. "Okay." This conversation wasn't going too well.

"The drawings look great! I'm so proud of you," Mom gushed. "Don't they, Mr. DeAndrews?"

"Quite," DeAndrews said, bending his lips in what I imagined was meant to be a smile. He looked like he had something smelly right under his nose. "I'm sure the folks in Happy Valley would find them utterly delightful."

He leaned in a little closer toward me.

"Didn't you get time to finish them?" he whispered. He waved his hand at my drawings. "Frankly, from what Mayor Coogan had told me, I was expecting a bit more than *doodles*. Drawings are so passé." Frost DeAndrews shuddered. "Maybe next time, dear boy, you should try some *ideas*— proper art. Hmm? Something that knocks me out of my socks. This whole trip is beginning to look like a complete waste of time."

Before I said something I might have regretted, Biff Coogan's voice came over the mike, welcoming everyone to the exhibition.

Just like his brother back in Happy Valley—I mean, Hills Valley— Biff Coogan liked the sound of his own voice. Next to me, Ellie checked her watch and then pulled me across to a quieter corner of the lobby.

"We'd better get into position," she said.

"You still think this is a good idea?" I whispered back.

"Why? Are you getting cold feet?" she said.

"No," I said, lying through my back teeth. I was more nervous than a sack full of turkeys on Christmas Eve. Then I thought of Frost DeAndrews. If nothing else, he would see what I'd really made for the exhibition. I hoped he had good socks on.

"Psst!" someone hissed close to my ear.

I turned to find myself looking at an asteroid.

A panel in the asteroid slid back to reveal Nico's face. "Ready?" he asked.

"An asteroid?" I said. "How do you go to the toilet dressed like that?"

"Never mind that!" Nico said. "Are you ready?"

I was still curious about the asteroid costume and the toilet problem, but I didn't push it. Nico was right—we had bigger fish to fry.

"Mikey and Dingbat are on standby," Nico reported. "Are we a go?"

I took a deep breath and nodded. "Let's do it."

CHAPTER 39

GO! GO! GO!

Sal's job was to cut the lights. She was positioned near the stairwell leading to the basement, where the fuse box was located. I saw her looking over at me and Ellie and Nico behind the curtains, waiting for the final go-ahead while Mayor Coogan droned on. Sal raised her eyebrows in a question.

I was about to give the thumbs-up to start things rolling when an image of Principal Stricker suddenly flashed into my mind.

If we did this thing, if we followed through with Operation R.O.C.K., Principal Stricker was *not* going to be happy. Nobody would be happy—not Mom, not the mayor, not a single one of the good citizens of Shark Bay other than The Outsiders—but it was the thought of how Principal Stricker would react that sent a shiver of pure fear trickling down my spine. I could feel her disapproval vibrating all the way across the Pacific.

Beware the mighty power of Stricker...

At that moment Ellie reached out and squeezed my hand. She must have known I was wobbling. I don't know how but she just did, and the touch of her hand gave me all the confidence I needed.

I gave Sal the thumbs-up. She nodded and ducked out of sight, down the stairwell. Stage One had begun.

"You ready?" Ellie said.

Before I could reply, all the lights went out in the lobby and we were plunged into blackness. There were a couple of jokey screams and a few people started laughing.

"Someone forgot to pay the power bill!" Kell shouted.

"At least it stopped the speeches!" someone else shouted.

"Initiate Stage Two," I whispered to Nico.

I heard some rustling in the dark as Nico fumbled for the switch hidden somewhere inside the asteroid. Nico was The Outsider's expert on lighting and sets. Mikey and Dingbat were in their positions in the basement, making sure we had power.

From under the bubbling water in the pool at
the foot of the waterfall, an eerie green light began
to glow. A thin mist drifted up from its surface.
Green shadows danced spookily across the walls
and the lobby grew strangely quiet. People began
to cluster around the edge of the pool.

"Wow," I whispered. "That looks great!"

"I went for the zombie-apocalypse look," Nico
replied.

"It's the end of the world!" Brad yelled, but no
one laughed.

"What on earth . . .?" I heard Biff Coogan say.

I saw Forest DeAndrew starting to look
interested for the first time all evening. It was
all the incentive I needed.

"Do it," I whispered to Ellie.

She picked up her remote control, thumbed the ON switch, and we moved to Stage Three of Operation R.O.C.K.

I ignored the voices inside my head on account of them being imaginary. That was the great thing about imaginary people.

Besides, it was too late to stop now.

CHAPTER 40

FREAK OUT!

The surface of the pool erupted and Ellie's bunyip, eyes glowing red and mouth gaping wide to reveal a row of fearsome razor-sharp choppers, came roaring up from the depths like a creature from your worst nightmare. And when it comes to nightmares, I'm something of an expert. Believe me, this one was an absolute doozy.

'*AWOOOOOOOOOOOOOOOOOOEEEEEEEEEEE-AAAARRGH!*' the bunyip bellowed, leaping into the lobby like it had spring-loaded feet. For all I knew that's exactly what it did have. Ellie had cranked the creature's voice up to ear-bleed level, and I could feel the vibrations in the pit of my stomach.

I'd known exactly what was going to come out of the pool and I still got such a shock I almost fainted.

I could only guess what effect the bunyip was having on everyone else.

I didn't have to wait long to find out.

'*Mommmmmmy!*' Brad squealed in a voice so loud and high-pitched that dogs in Sydney started barking.

Brad turned and ran like he was being chased by a flesh-eating zombie bunyip, which, as far as he was concerned, he was. In his blind panic, he ran straight into one of the temporary toilets, breaking a pipe and sending a geyser of brown goop all over his perfect hair.

I knew those toilets were going to come into this somewhere.

The rest of The Surf Gorillas
weren't doing much better than Brad.
I saw a couple of them flat-out faint
while Belinda did her best to climb
a large potted palm in an attempt to
get away.

Operation R.O.C.K. was working. Brad
had been publicly humiliated. Revenge
was mine!

Except for one teeny-tiny detail.

When I'd planned this whole thing,
the idea was that it would be Brad—
and Brad alone—in the firing line.
Everyone else in Australia's Most
Fearless Town would quickly see that the
bunyip was a joke, wouldn't they? Ha, ha, ha . . .?

Khatchadorian, you're such a joker, mate!

Australians liked practical jokes, right? Hadn't Kell told me to lighten up? Rafe Khatchadorian's Great Practical Joke would be the funniest thing to have ever happened in Shark Bay. Right?

Wrong.

Everyone F-R-E-A-K-E-D.

Not just Brad.

Everyone.

CHAPTER 41

OOPS

Wailing like a police siren, the astronaut leapt off the lobby balcony, landing heavily on a herd of stampeding Elvis dental technicians from the Shark Bay Dental Clinic.

Nearby, six Salvador Dali's from the Shark
Bay Surrealist Society were trampled underfoot
by a bevy of beefy ballerinas from the Bayside
Bowls Team. A Viking, a Roman centurion,
Frost DeAndrews, and a guy in a giant teddy-bear
costume were doing their best to hide under the
skirts of a howling Queen Victoria while, to my left,
an unconscious Darth Vader was being lifted to
safety by a baby with a beard. Biff Coogan shinned
up an ornamental pillar, accidentally disturbing a
wasps' nest near the lobby ceiling with disastrous
results.

A group of pandas were fighting each other to get out of the emergency exit.

It was pandamonium.

Everywhere was screaming and running and panic and destruction. Things had got out of hand.

"Kill the bunyip!" I shouted to Ellie. "We have to stop it!"

Ellie wrestled with the remote. "I can't! It's not responding!"

Nico, Sal, Ellie, and I looked helplessly at the bunyip. Little snakes of electricity ran up and down its body, and sparks began shooting from gaps in the creature's skin. It lumbered across the flooded lobby floor, its roar getting louder and louder with every step.

We had created a monster.

CHAPTER 42

LASER-BEAM EYES

The only silver lining to this out-of-control Frankenstein scenario was the reaction of Kell Weathers.

The very second Kell glimpsed the bunyip, he dropped his glass, let out a scream almost as high-pitched as Brad's, and hurled Mom toward the creature before turning on his heel and sprinting for the exit.

Mom bounced off the bunyip and came to rest on the soaking-wet lobby floor, her face a picture

Outta my Way!

of anger and disgust as she watched Kell carve a path of yellow-bellied destruction.

I wasn't happy that my mom had been treated so badly, but I was kind of glad that she had finally seen Kell for what he really was. If I was going to get in trouble for this (and something told me I was going to get in more trouble for this than for anything I had ever done in my life), then Mom seeing Kell's gigantic yellow streak would go some way to making it all worthwhile. She really did deserve better than Kell Weathers.

As if reading my thoughts, her head swiveled toward me (I swear it rotated 180 degrees) and, although it was absolutely impossible for her to have spotted me in the shadows behind the curtains, she zapped a full-strength laser-beam mom stare in my direction.

sizzLe!

In that split second I knew that she knew.

How do they do that? Moms, I mean. Is there a special training school? A secret set of mom skills handed to them when you're born?

It's all in here, Mrs Khatchadorian. Everything you need to know. Read it and then burn it. We can't allow it to fall into the wrong hands.

I sank back into the shadows as Mom got to her feet. This was it. I was about to start a life sentence of being grounded.

But, just as I began to move, Mom suddenly turned and stalked out of the lobby.

I let out a long breath that I didn't know I'd been holding in. I felt like I'd dodged a bullet, but one thing was for sure—if Mom ever found out for certain that I was the mastermind behind all this, I was toast.

CHAPTER 43

LIFE'S A GAS

Sixty seconds after the bunyip first appeared there was no one left in the lobby apart from me and The Outsiders. Even The Surf Gorillas who had fainted had managed to crawl off into the night. Mayor Coogan had slid down his pole and disappeared. There was no sign of Frost DeAndrews or Marie Antoinette or my mom, and not a single ballerina, Elvis, pirate, punk, dinosaur, boxer, or bear was to be seen.

Crackling like an out-of-tune radio, the bunyip lurched unsteadily across a floor littered with fancy-dress props—false teeth, wigs, eyeglasses, hats, a wooden pirate's leg, a stuffed parrot, the head of a panda. An abandoned camera had jammed and it flashed at odd intervals, making

the lobby look as though there was a lightning
storm outside.

"Anything?" I asked Ellie, who was still fiddling
with the remote.

She shook her head. "It's like it's got a mind of
its own."

The bunyip reached the opposite side of the
lobby, hit the wall, then turned toward the open
door. Flames began to lick upwards through holes
in the creature's skin.

Sal grabbed a fire extinguisher off the wall. "Well, we can't let it burn the place down."

"Hold on a second, Sal," Ellie said. "It's heading outside."

"There's not too much damage in here," Nico said. "Some water on the floor and a few broken glasses. We could disappear. No one knows it was us."

I had a sudden flashback to Mom looking in my direction when the bunyip appeared. Was I really sure she knew? Or was that just guilt talking? Whatever, Nico's idea was definitely worth considering. Deny everything. Let the bunyip become one of those urban myths.

SHARK BAY BULLETIN

MYSTERY MONSTER! AUTHORITIES BAFFLED!

"LIKE A GIANT MUTANT FROG!" SAY LOCALS

POSSIBLE UFO LINK?

"Look," Mikey said.

The bunyip had made it outside and started to put some distance between it and the surf club. Good. Every step it took meant less danger and less chance of us being found out. It looked like we were going to be okay.

We followed the bunyip outside and watched it stagger toward the splintered remains of the toilet Brad had smashed up. It was almost completely on fire now and moving much more slowly. Every so often it made a little electronic beep or squawk, which somehow made it sound weirdly alive. It was like it knew it was dying.

"Maybe the best thing is to let it burn out," Nico said. "Destroy the evidence?"

"Yes," I said. "It's probably the be—"

Chemistry isn't something I pay much attention to but, as the bunyip crossed the last few feet to the smashed toilet block, one word leapt into my mind like a great big flashing neon sign: METHANE.

"Run!" I yelled.

CHAPTER 44

BOOM!

"Methane," Mr. Hernandez said—yep, the very same Mr. Hernandez whose mustache I'd yanked all those pages ago—"is a very combustible gas."

When he was covering science one day, he showed us a film about methane that had been trapped underground and was the cause of a

Methane production unit

PARP!

terrible mining disaster. Methane, Mr. Hernandez told us, was produced by rotting vegetation, by the underground release of gas from coal seams, by rice fields, by the digestion systems of cows . . . and from the rear ends of human beings. We'd all laughed at that, which was probably why I'd remembered it.

A toilet block was more or less a collecting station for methane, and we had a flaming bunyip on a collision course for one right now.

It was too late for Sal's fire extinguisher.

It was too late to try to fix the remote control.

It was too late to do anything except get out of Dodge and do it *now*.

As the bunyip stepped into the toilet block, we turned and ran for our lives. I had no idea how big a methane explosion could be, so I ran about as fast as I have ever run in my life. Every step would take me a little closer to saf—

The universe exploded behind me in a blast of orange light, and I was thrown head first through the air.

CHAPTER 45

STARING DEATH RIGHT IN THE FACE

The Grim Reaper's long shadow covered me as he took a couple of steps forward, his heavy scythe sliding across the dry grass. My feet were glued to the floor. When the black-clad figure was no more than a scythe-length away, he lifted an arm and a long white finger pointed directly at me.

"Rafe Khatchadorian," the Grim Reaper said, his voice like dust.

"This time you have

gone too far. Your time as the Hills Valley art representative has come to an end. Your career as an artist is over before it even started. It is time to pay the piper."

My mouth went dry. I tried to say something but I couldn't. Besides, what could I say? Sorry? Did the Grim Reaper have a court of appeal?

The Grim Reaper ran a finger along the scythe before pushing back the hood of the robe to reveal a familiar face.

"Mom?" I said.

"No, it's me."

I opened my eyes to see Ellie's face floating above me.

"Can you hear me?"

"You're floating," I said.

"No," Ellie said. "I'm not. You're lying in a ditch."

Ellie had clearly lost her mind, and I was about to tell her exactly that when I realized she was right. I *was* lying in a ditch. I couldn't remember getting there or why I would be there. I don't even like ditches.

And then it all came back to me, just like that. Bunyip. Fire. Explosion.

Ellie, Nico, Sal, Mikey, and Dingbat came into view. Mikey's eyebrows were singed and Dingbat's head was smoking but, other than that, they seemed fine.

I got to my feet, brushed off the worst of the dirt, and breathed a sigh of relief. This was bad—really bad—but at least I hadn't killed anyone.

"Everyone okay?" I said.

"We're fine," Dingbat replied, "except you did have your butt in my face when we landed."

"You had *your* butt in *my* face," Ellie said with a shudder.

"We're all good," Nico said. "No one hurt."

We staggered up to the top of the embankment and stood in silence, watching a great plume of fire and smoke rising from what remained of the toilets and our zombie bunyip.

"Woah," Dingbat said.

Woah was right. Woah just about covered all bases.

Lightning zigzagged across the sky, followed closely by a crack of thunder. The storm that had been threatening earlier was about to hit.

I glanced up just as a fat raindrop landed on my

head. Within three seconds the skies had opened
and the heaviest rain I had ever seen came down.
The fire spat and hissed and then went out like
someone had thrown a giant bucket of water over
it. In the distance I could see red and blue flashing
lights heading our way.

You know how in movies, at moments like this,
someone always comes up with a smart line that
sums everything up and is kinda cool and tough
at the same time?

That doesn't happen in real life.

CHAPTER 46

WHO, ME?

It took Shark Bay exactly twenty-two minutes to figure out who was behind The Great Surf Club Zombie Bunyip Disaster.

The first hint that no one was going to believe we were innocent came when I arrived back at the Coogans' place. I had hoped to slink in unnoticed under the cover of darkness. I was soaked to the bone and all I wanted to do was have a shower, get dry, and get into bed.

Instead, everyone was gathered in the living room waiting for me when I opened the door.

All eyes turned to me as I stood there, dripping all over the shag pile and trying not to look guilty—which, if you've ever tried it, you'll know is a hard look to pull off when you are innocent. When you're actually guilty, it's practically impossible.

"Oh," I said. "Hi, everyone."

Brad, wrapped in a blanket, gave me a look of pure hatred.

Ditto Belinda.

Ditto everyone except, maybe, Mom.

She gave me a look that combined suspicion, shame, anger, fear, and relief. You'd think *that* would be a hard one to manage but she did it without blinking. Another one of those mom skills, I guess.

"Do you have something to say to us, Rafe?" Biff said.

Barb stood next to him, her arms folded.

Did I? I didn't know. Other than an exploded toilet block and a spoiled exhibition, there was no real harm done, was there?

"You know Brad was injured?" Mom said.

I looked at Brad. "What happened?"

"He ran into the woods to get away from whatever that was back there," Barb said, "and got bitten by a possum."

"Doesn't sound too bad," I said.

"That depends where you get bitten," Brad whimpered. "I might need a rabies shot!"

I tried not to smile. It was difficult. The idea of a possum giving cowardly Brad a nip in the privates was just about the funniest

thing I'd ever heard. And if anyone deserved a rabies shot it was Brad Coogan. I wrestled with my lips but couldn't stop the smallest smirk from appearing.

"Any sign of Kell?" I asked Mom.

She shook her head. Only an expert on Jules (like me) could tell that Mom was about two seconds away from bursting into tears. My mini-smile disappeared like snow on a griddle. I walked over and gave her a hug.

"I'm sure he'll be fine," I said.

Mom nodded and sniffed. "I hope not," she said, and we both smiled. Mom walked to the kitchen and I headed upstairs.

That hadn't been so bad. They were all suspicious, but it wasn't like anyone had any *proof*.

That's when the mob of zombies arrived.

CHAPTER 47

THERE'S NO REASONING
WITH AN ANGRY MOB
OF ZOMBIES

Okay, this is where we started, so it might be worth reminding everyone of the situation.

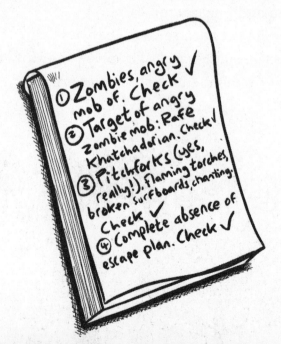

① Zombies, angry mob of. Check ✓
② Target of angry zombie mob: Rafe Khatchadorian. Check ✓
③ Pitchforks (yes, really!), flaming torches, broken surfboards, chanting. Check ✓
④ Complete absence of escape plan. Check ✓

I said my prayers and hoped that the mob would stop short of actually killing me, but I couldn't rule it out. The only crumb of comfort I had was that the zombie mob weren't real zombies, just an entire town of enraged partygoers who had been frightened half to death by an animatronic bunyip.

Maybe they'd just give me a very stern lecture and tell me not to do it again. Maybe when they got real close they'd see that deep down I was a nice guy and they'd rethink their plans for bloody retribution.

Or, then again, maybe they wouldn't.

And they were just a few of the *nicer* things they said. Some of the more colorful ones can't be repeated here. A woman dressed as Tinkerbell, who I recognized as the local librarian, was swearing so much I thought her head was going to explode.

Brad had got most of the poop off, but I noticed that most of the other zombies were standing a few paces away from him. It was like he'd activated some sort of poop force field. I was pretty sure that wouldn't do anything to improve his mood. Belinda also didn't look like she was ready to forgive anything. Being puked on, she had more against me than most, I guess.

"Oh boy," Leo muttered. "This is worse than I thought."

"Gee, is that supposed to cheer me up?" I turned around but Leo had vanished. Even my imaginary brother had chickened out.

I leaned closer to the window and saw Biff Coogan below me, standing outside his front door arguing with the ringleaders. I couldn't hear much of what Biff was saying but I think he was pointing out that, while I probably deserved anything they were suggesting as punishment, he, Biffly Algernon Coogan, Mayor of Shark Bay, could not stand by and watch his guest being torn limb from limb.

"Think of the publicity!" Biff reasoned. "And the mess! The police will want to know what happened to him."

"No, they won't!" a man dressed as a punk rocker said. "I'm Sergeant Dick Dooley and most of the department is already here."

"And the Fire Department," someone else shouted.

"Everyone's here, Biff!" Sergeant Dooley said. "So let us at the little blot, and we'll see he gets what's coming!"

Biff was clearly jolted by the unexpected appearance of the Shark Bay Police Department in the zombie mob but he did a good job of not letting it show. He crossed his arms and jutted out his chin defiantly. "Now, that might be the case, Dick, but it's still no way for a town to b—"

"There he is!" Brad squealed like a pig that had found a trench full of slops.

Everyone looked up at me, and the effect was like dropping a match on a petrol-soaked bonfire. A great roar rose from the mob and all the pitchforks and flaming torches and surfboard splinters were lifted in the air. The zombies pushed Biff aside like he was made of straw and swarmed toward the door.

I was doomed.

CHAPTER 48

MIGHTY MOM

"**S**top right there!"

A voice split the night air. It was like an atomic bomb going off, and it stopped the mob dead in its tracks. It was a voice that demanded to be obeyed. It was the voice of authority.

It was the voice of Mom the All-Powerful.

I leaned over the rail of the balcony and looked down at the Coogan hallway below.

Mom, wearing her superhero costume and a steely expression, faced down the mob. She stood toe to toe with Sergeant Dooley, her hands on her hips.

"No one move a muscle," Mom snarled. She jabbed the cop in the chest with a finger. "If anyone so much as *touches* my kid, they'll have *me* to deal with. Understand?"

Now, I'm not a teenager who cries much but
I have to admit my eyes welled up seeing my mom
like this. There wasn't a tiger on earth who would
have protected her cub with more determination or
sharper claws. If Dooley and the rest of the zombie
mob knew what was good for them they'd quit now.

"He's made a fool of us all!" Dooley barked.
"He's got to pay!"

Behind him, the mob muttered agreement.

"He's made a fool of Shark Bay!" a voice yelled
from the back.

"I hate him!" Brad declared.

"He puked on me!" Belinda shouted.

A few of the mob did double-takes as if they hadn't heard right. Not only was this guy a slimy bunyip-releaser, I could hear them thinking, he's also a lowlife girl-puker-onner?

"And these pitchforks cost money!" someone else piped up.

Mom stepped forward. "First, there's no proof that Rafe was involved in *anything*."

I gulped. Mom was on thin ice here. *I* was on thin ice.

CRACK!

One false move and the mob would push her aside and start handing out some homemade justice. But Mom wasn't finished, not by a long shot.

"Secondly," she said, raising her voice, "if he *was* involved, then he *has* made a fool of you all." Mom's voice got sharper, something I hadn't believed possible until I heard it for myself. It had an edge to it that could have sharpened a scimitar. "And I imagine the rest of Australia would be very interested to see exactly how 'Australia's Most Fearless Town' ran away from a rubber *toy*."

I could almost see everyone's brains working as they processed the information. Mom was right. If this got out, Shark Bay would become a laughing stock.

Dick Dooley narrowed his eyes. "Are you threatening us?"

"That's rich," Mom said, "coming from someone holding a pitchfork and standing at the head of a bunch of angry zombies."

She had a point.

"But, yes, since you mention it," she continued, "it *is* a threat. Now get off my property!"

Technically, it was Biff and Barb Coogan's property, but we all knew what she meant.

"No one will believe you bunch of blow-ins!" Dooley said. "Where's your proof?"

"Right here.' Ellie stepped forward and held up her phone so the mob could see.

"Where did *you* come from?" I said.

"Never mind that now," Ellie hissed. Her finger hovered over her phone screen. "If I press this button, the evidence will be uploaded to the internet. Everyone will know you all ran!"

"How?" Sergeant Dooley asked.

Ellie smiled. "I filmed the whole thing."

CHAPTER 49

THE TRUTH ABOUT
ELLIE'S CLIP

"**W**e planted cameras around the surf club," Ellie said smugly. "I just spent the last hour editing, and now it's waiting to be uploaded to my video channel. I just need to press one little button." She paused dramatically and eyeballed the mob. "Of course, in all the excitement, I might have accidentally deleted most of the clip."

She looked down at Dooley, who, it seemed, had assumed the role of leader of the (almost) zombie mob.

"So what you have to ask yourself is: Are you feeling lucky? Well, are you, punk?"

It turned out he wasn't.

And neither was the rest of the zombie mob. They lowered their pitchforks and flaming torches and surfboard fins. Faced with a choice between global humiliation and revenge on me (assuming they could get past the Mom of Steel) and backing down, the mob chose to back down. One by one they began to drift off into the rainswept darkness.

"Were you really going to download the clip?" I whispered.

Ellie lowered her phone and smiled. "What clip?"

CHAPTER 50

KANGAROOS SUCK

If you don't mind, I'll skip over the rest of my time in Shark Bay as quickly as possible.

It wasn't pleasant.

Mom postponed any action over my possible involvement in the Great Zombie Bunyip Disaster until we were home.

The Coogans treated us well enough for the remainder of our stay—by which I mean they treated us like we were radioactive. The weather may have been hot outside but the temperature at 22 Sunspot Crescent was arctic. The cultural exchange experiment between Hills Valley and Shark Bay had been a total disaster.

I didn't even see Brad or Belinda again, which was just fine by me. I would happily spend the rest

of my life never seeing either of the twins again,
and they must have felt exactly the same. In that
way, and that way alone, we had something in
common.

After having time to think about it, I decided
that it had been worth it. No one had been badly
injured (unless you counted Brad having his
privates nibbled by a possum), no real damage
had been done (other than one exploded temporary
toilet block), and I had hit back for being almost

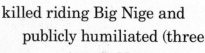

killed riding Big Nige and publicly humiliated (three times!). Not to mention The Surf Gorillas getting punished for wrecking *Revenge of the Teenage Zombie Bunyip From Mars*. And there was the little matter of Kell vanishing.

All in all, I reflected, they had deserved what they'd got.

And Ellie and The Outsiders?

Ellie and I talked until late that night. I won't tell you what we said or how we left it. That's just for me and Ellie. Meeting The Outsiders had been the highlight of my trip. I wouldn't forget them or regret a single thing about coming to Australia.

Except not seeing a kangaroo. I hadn't seen a single one of those overgrown hoppy rats.

Now, *that* sucked.

CHAPTER 51

ATTACK OF THE
FIFTY-FOOT
CONSCIENCE MONSTER

I'm sorry about Kell," I said to Mom. "I mean,
I did think he was a total jerk and all, but
I know you liked him. I shouldn't have been so
pleased when he . . . you know . . ."

"When he showed what a coward he was?" Mom
said. "When he threw me in the way of the bunyip
and ran for his life, screaming like a three-year-old
who'd seen the bogeyman?"

"Maybe that's what geologists are like," I offered.

"I don't think so, Rafe. I'm sure there are plenty
of brave geologists out there. Just not Kell."

"Anyway," I said, "you liked him and I'm sorry
I made him do what he did.'

We were 38,000 feet above the Pacific Ocean, about halfway back to Hills Valley.

Mom shrugged. "I thought I liked him, but he turned out to be someone different to who I thought he was. I suppose I can thank you for that. But I'm fine, honestly, Rafe. Just fine."

Mom put her headphones back in and started watching a movie. I noticed that none of her lucky charms were visible and that she seemed pretty calm for someone terrified of flying. I guess that after everything that had gone on in Shark Bay, a flight back home didn't seem like such a big deal.

I sat back in my seat and listened to the sound of the engines.

I was home free. So why didn't I feel better?

The answer came to me somewhere over Hawaii. There was the obvious stuff like missing Ellie and the rest of the guys, but that wasn't it. No, what was bugging me was that we—me and The Outsiders—had done something *great*, something really difficult, and no one outside Shark Bay would ever know.

And we never got to make our film.

CHAPTER 52

I WAS A
TEENAGE OUTSIDER
(AND I LIKED IT)

I did get grounded. But that was fair. I deserved it.

I *had* ruined the trip. I had to be punished. The only question was: How much?

I talked to Ellie a few times online. She mentioned she might make a trip to Hills Valley before too long. "And I'm working on something. Keep an eye on the post, okay?" she'd added.

I tried to get her to say more but she wouldn't. Nothing much had changed for her in Shark Bay.

"We were always The Outsiders," she'd said. "That's the way I like it too."

That was a good way of looking at things. I was kind of an outsider at Hills Valley. The thing was, before I met Ellie and the rest of The Outsiders, I'd always seen that as a negative. Perhaps I'd been looking at things the wrong way. Instead of trying to fit in with everyone else, maybe I'd be better off *not* fitting in and liking it.

I've started getting more interested in filmmaking, too. I've even begun working on storyboards for my own movie. A horror movie, of course.

Best of all, I realized something important the trip had taught me. It was something my mom said in between telling me how grounded I was. She'd said that bravery came in many forms and she thought I was brave for producing art.

"At least you're trying," she'd said. "You might be scared of sharks and snakes and imaginary drop bears, but who isn't?"

She stopped short of actually saying she approved of me letting an animatronic zombie bunyip loose on Shark Bay, but that was never going to happen.

Being back home felt good. On the upside, it was great to see Grandma Dotty. On the downside, I was back under the same roof as Georgia.

Only kidding.

There was one really great thing about being back in Hills Valley. As my feet slid between the sheets I was pretty sure that there wouldn't be any snakes.

Total contentment

THE END.

CHAPTER 53

AN ARTIST LIKE KHATCHADORIAN

Wait!

Something else happened. Probably the best thing to come out of the whole trip (apart from meeting Ellie).

Four weeks after arriving back I got something in the post marked with Australian stamps.

Inside it was a magazine and a note from Ellie. All it said was: PAGES 32–4.

I carefully unrolled the magazine. It was something called *The Great Australian Art Monthly*—a big, thick glossy thing

full of articles about famous Australian artists and artists from other places visiting Australia.

I flicked to page 32 and almost passed out.

It was a picture of the bunyip ripping through the lobby of the Shark Bay Surf Club. It had been taken on a phone camera and was a little fuzzy but it still looked awesome. The bunyip's mouth was open and sparks were shooting out. The photo had caught lots of people screaming and running. "Zombie Movie Art Triumph at Shark Bay by Frost DeAndrews" read the headline.

"I thought I had been fooled," DeAndrews wrote, "when the *Zombie Movie* exhibition I had been invited to at sleepy little Shark Bay turned out to be nothing more than a collection of passable sketches by visiting young American artist Rafe Khatchadorian.

"Boy, was I wrong. In one of the most scintillating and brave performance art productions I have seen in recent years, Khatchadorian and his art group, The Outsiders, ran us right through the A–Z of contemporary art and treated us to a totally immersive experience not seen since the days of Wilhelm Van Purpleschpittel and the Neo-Colonial Burble Movement . . ."

The rest of the article was illustrated with more photos of the whole event and interviews with Ellie and the guys and a lot of artspeak I didn't understand. Even Mayor Coogan got in on the act.

"Rafe insisted on keeping everything top secret," he said. "We're very proud of Shark Bay's association with an artist like Khatchadorian."

An artist like Khatchadorian.

It had a ring to it. I liked it.

"Mom!" I shouted, leaping off my bed. "You gotta see this!"

EPILOGUE

Tasty?

Not bad. It was a geologist I found in the woods. Ran right into me.

Um, it might be a good idea to point out that this is a metaphor. No geologists were hurt during the making of this story.

ABOUT THE AUTHOR

JAMES PATTERSON is the internationally bestselling author of the highly praised Middle School books, *Homeroom Diaries*, and the I Funny, Treasure Hunters, Confessions, Maximum Ride, Witch & Wizard and Daniel X series. James Patterson has been the most borrowed author in UK libraries for the past seven years in a row and his books have sold more than 300 million copies worldwide, making him one of the bestselling authors of all time. He lives in Florida.

MARTIN CHATTERTON was born in Liverpool, England and has been successfully writing and illustrating books for almost thirty years. He has written dozens of children's books and illustrated many more for other writers, including several British Children's Laureates. His work has been published in fourteen languages and has won and been shortlisted in numerous awards in the UK, US, and Australia. Alongside writing for children, Martin writes crime fiction (as Ed Chatterton), continues to work as a graphic designer, and is currently working on his PhD. After time spent in the US, Martin now divides his time between Australia and the UK.